THE JOURNEY OF BARBRAH ROSE

Shaun Gresham

authorHOUSE®

AuthorHouse™
1663 Liberty Drive
Bloomington, IN 47403
www.authorhouse.com
Phone: 1 (800) 839-8640

Published by AuthorHouse 04/29/2020

ISBN: 978-1-7283-6040-9 (sc)
ISBN: 978-1-7283-6039-3 (e)

PROLOGUE

God is so good.

I sit in my Nashville condo, looking through a photo album. I usually don't like thinking of the past, but for some reason, I feel compelled to think of it. I opened the album and the first photo that catches my eye features me at the age of five, Aunt Katherine, and my mother. Aunt Katherine and I were showing our pearly white smiles. It's one of the rare times that I got to see my mother during my childhood. I can recall that moment like it was yesterday. Me being a precocious five-year-old left in the tender loving hands of Aunt Katherine. My mother came to visit us, but she was sloppy drunk.

"What are you feeding this child?" I recalled my mother asking Aunt Katherine when she saw me.

"Don't you dare come to my house talking about my baby like that!" I remembered Aunt Katherine replying to my mother's question.

"This is my child! "Mother yelled as she grabbed my arm.

"A child you hardly visit much less takes care of." Aunt Katherine proclaimed as she pushes my mother away from me.

Another photo has me, Aunt Katherine, and legendary gospel singer Shirley Norman. In the picture, I was thirteen years old, wearing a pink dress that Aunt Katherine made. We're at a gospel concert where I was the opening act and Shirley Norman was the closing act. Right before we took this picture, Ms. Norman gave me some encouraging words about my singing ability.

There's another photo of me and my first boyfriend, Derik McFarland. He was a straight-up dog. I was sixteen and he was seventeen. We dated for a year until he graduated high school and enlisted in the military.

Then the last photo in the album has me in my graduation gown with my high school diploma. I see the excitement I exhibited in the picture. A life full of promises and possibilities.

CHAPTER ONE

"We will be contacting you once we make our decision."

"Thanks for your time." I say back to the producers of the upcoming gospel musical "*I Swear on My Pastor's Cranberry Juice,*" which will be produced in September at the Atlantic Civic Center. I think I did a pretty good audition if I say so myself. Two thousand and thirteen people showed up for the auditions, and I am No. 24. I stood out, especially with my cobalt blue blazer outfit, which I paid fifteen dollars for at a yard sale. Getting valuables at low prices is an art I learned from my Aunt Katherine. That woman can hold on to a nickel like soap on a washcloth. To this day, Aunt Katherine refuses to shop at Rich's or Macy's. Wal-Mart and the Thrift Store are her favorite stores to shop. Also, I'm grateful that she encouraged me to save all the earnings that I got as a gospel vocalist. Because of her, I know how to make clothes, which is a great asset to have, mainly because I'm a full-figured sexy woman.

"Excuse me." A voice says behind me as I prepared to exit the building.

"Yes sir." I answer the nasal voice gentleman in a tone of frustration. He kind of reminds me of Danny Devito.

Hi, my name is Nicholas Sphere; I am a talent manager

and one of my clients, Wanda Bash is holding auditions for background singers and I must say you have an awesome voice. "So, here's my card, please feel free to give me a call and set up and appointment with my secretary." After Mr. Sphere left, I immediately went to the nearest payphone and dialed the contact info on the card he gave. I would be a fool not to take the opportunity to work with Wanda Bash. She's regarded as soul music royalty. Growing up, I would listen to her music, or rather I had to sneak and listen to her music because I wasn't allowed listening to secular music while growing up. I did enjoy listening to it at my friend's house though.

My appointment is set at 2 pm on Thursday. Wanda Bash, here I come. When I got home, I had to prepare the outfit that I was going to wear and the song that I was going to sing. I know one thing, the hot weather in Atlanta is not kind to me, especially if you must sit in it to wait for the bus. It seems like I have to sit for eternity to catch a bus. A Middle Eastern woman, whose body is fully covered in a black cloth, was sitting next to me. I wonder how she manages to survive the hot weather with that kind of attire. If I was her, I would attach a small air condition unit under those garments. I start thinking about the Church of God in Christ Church, which is the denomination I was raised in. I wasn't allowed to wear pants, makeup, and fingernail polish. Going to the movies is considered sinful. Right now, I want to get home and relax in my air-conditioned apartment and watch my soaps.

I've been in Atlanta for two months, and it's been a struggle finding work. I briefly had a gig at an exclusive four-star hotel, but they let me go because I couldn't conform to losing weight. The only thing I'm going to miss about the hotel is the scrumptious meals and the luxurious hotel rooms. Now I got to budget my money to buy some groceries.

Thank goodness the bus finally arrives, but it appears to be crowded. I'm just anxious to get home and unwind. As I board the bus, some of the patrons stare superciliously. I'm used to getting that kind of stare. Because the bus is full, I must remain standing. As I'm standing, I look at the hair care advertisements plaster on the bus windows. It would be nice if those ads feature full-figured women like me.

"Oh, look at that fat cow." I hear a female voice yell. I turn around, and my eyes lay upon this dark skin female. She's very androgynous, wearing baggy clothing and hi-tech boots. "Yeah, I'm talking to you." She boldly exclaims.

"I got your cow little girl." "Oh, excuse me." "I meant little boy." Some of my fellow patrons started laughing.

"We can get off the bus and get it on Queen Kong."

"Oh, you don't want to mess with me."

The Bible scripture that my Aunt Katherine used to quote for me says, "the weapons of my warfare are not carnal." But the opposite is about to occur. We manage to get off at the next stop in front of a local shopping plaza, which was close to where I live.

"You know what I don't like fat chicks like you. I'm afraid you might cause the earth to collapse."

"You know what I don't like your foul breath; it will make my face collapse."

Then the little roach pushes me. I, in turn, threw a right hook to her left jaw. She immediately falls to the ground.

"Now that's what I call a collapse and if you have any more problems, I don't mind hitting you on your right jaw."

As I walked home, I saw a familiar face. Low and behold, it was Mr. Hellmann's sitting on the street corner belting the Blues.

This man keeps showing up everywhere. I can't get away from him it seems. In my years of singing, this man occasionally shows up out of nowhere.

After handling the dead weight, the five-minute walk home is easy, but living in Techwood Homes isn't. Techwood Home is the first housing project established in the US during the Great Depression. Something that was intended to be a help up turned out to be a letdown. Complacency is what occupies the lives of the inhabitants of Techwood. My neighbors Robert and LuAnn Johnson are one of the casualties. They have been here for almost thirty years since their early twenties. Robert works at Mead while LuAnn is a housewife. They raised six kids in Techwood, and they treat me as if I'm one of their own.

"Hey baby, how did the audition go?" Luann asks in her sweet Betty Rubble voice as she sweeps near her door area.

"I got a chance to audition for Wanda Bash."

"I told you that God's going to work it out for you. Why don't you come on in here and let me fix you some lunch?"

I never say no to LuAnn's meals. Her cooking reminds me of Aunt Katherine's. Her shrimp casserole is to die for. I love her homemade lemon pound cake. She can give Ms. Winners a run for her money when it comes to making fried chicken. I'm glad to call the Johnson good friends of mine. I walk into her apartment and as always, it's immaculate. The inside of this place doesn't look like your typical home from the projects. I'm glad LuAnn doesn't use plastic covers over the couch, unlike most people from her generation.

"Girl I'm going to fix you my famous sliced ham and turkey sandwich with French fries." LuAnn happily states as she puts her apron on.

"How was your day LuAnn"? I ask as I sit at the dining table.

"It was okay until Miss Thang came over here asking me for some money."

"You must be talking about Tasha Hayes."

"Yes ma'am. I had to cuss her out good. She is always going around, asking folks for money to feed her drug habit. She needs to get herself a job and start being a mother to her kids."

"Yeah, she called me a fat whore the other day because I refused to give her any money. I almost slapped that girl."

"She's just liked her mother, who I had to beat up when she tried to flirt with my husband. The apple doesn't fall too far from the tree."

"Yeah seem like the whole family is pitiful."

"The Hayes has been in Techwood just as long as we have. We have been dealing with them for too long."

It won't be long before I'm out of this Techwood dump.

Hopefully, working with Wanda Bash will be my shot of getting my foot into the door of showbiz. Wanda will have the opportunity to hear me, and I know she's going to hire me. I know I'm talented. As I think about some of the established singers who kicked off their careers singing behind someone else. People like Luther Vandross and Whitney Houston. Songwriters Burt Bacharach and Hal

5

David discovered Dionne Warwick in the studio recording background vocals for the Drifters. Mariah Carey, the new singer that just came out, started her career singing behind Brenda K. Starr. Whitney's mom, Cissy, and Darlene Love have made careers as a background vocalist. Darlene briefly had a few hit records of her own in the early sixties but found contentment in the studio. I eventually want a career in the foreground.

Recently I got a three-day gig at Club Clooney's a jazz joint in College Park. The club is sophisticated and classy. The owner remembers me from the hotel gig. I will have the opportunity to perform the same kind of songs Billie Holiday, Ella Fitzgerald, and Sarah Vaughn sang. Right now, my focus is getting ready for my Wanda Bash audition. Gretchen, my good friend from back home, will help me get ready for my audition. I think that's her ringing the doorbell now.

"Hey, Gretchen!"

"Hi, Bobbi!"

Gretchen stands before me, looking like she just stepped off the cover of Vogue magazine. She could give Cindy Crawford a run for her money. I met Gretchen during my gospel circuit days. She's a professional dancer who was romantically involved with my former manager and pastor. As we embraced, I thought about the times Gretchen encourages me to pursue an R&B career and move to Atlanta. She is the only friend who doesn't condescendingly look down on me because of my weight.

"Bobbi, I love this 40's outfit you're wearing. I think this would be a good outfit for your audition, but I'm going to help you with your makeup and hair."

"Girl, you don't know anything about handling black hair."

"Like whatever. I have your hair looking like Whitney Houston's. After your audition, I'm taking you out for lunch so we can talk."

Two hours later, I'm at Bash Over the Head Studios, which is owned by Wanda. I am totally nervous. In all the years I've been performing, I've never step foot into a recording studio. When I was sixteen, Sam Collins, my manager, secured a record deal for me to record a gospel album. Two weeks after signing the contract, I was supposed to report to the studio to record my first album. I had chosen and rehearse the songs I wanted to record. I was very excited. Three hours before my recording time, I saw the owner of the record label on the news being arrested for fraud and drug trafficking. That incident really put a bad taste in my mouth about the gospel industry. Also, I began to see the worm that Rev. Dr. Bishop Sam Collins is. That was two years ago; now I stand in the lobby of a recording studio owned by one of the biggest singing stars of the century. The first person I encounter is the receptionist who is sitting at the desk, giving me that "who you are and what do you want look."

"May I help you?" She asks me in her sassy Ebonics vernacular.

"Yes, I have an appointment with Miss. Bash."

"Okay, go ahead and have a seat, someone will be with you shortly."

I found myself a seat but can't sit for long. I began to become fixated and amazed at all the pictures I see on the wall. I looked at the photos Wanda took with people from MLK, to MC Hammer, and many other influential people.

"Hello, my beautiful songbird."

I turn around and saw Mr. Sphere behind me, beaming showing his megawatt smile.

"Thank you so much for giving me the opportunity to audition before Miss. Bash."

"No, Thank You for showing up you are so talented, and Miss Bash will be knocked out by your voice."

"You are too kind Mr. Sphere," I say to him as we walk arm and arm.

"Wanda and her vocal coach are waiting for you in studio C. You go in and break a leg."

OMG, this is my big chance. As I was walking into the studio, all kinds of questions were rambling in my brain. Will I be told I'm fat? Will I be told my outfit is wrong? Will I be told that I performed the wrong song? I took a deep breath and walked towards destiny.

Chapter Two

"It's okay, Bobbi. Wanda Bash is not the only singer in the world who need background singers. It's been two weeks since your audition and you're still fretting over it. Remember you're already a working singer. They extended your gig at club Clooney's, so you need to get a grip on yourself." Gretchen says as I drown my sorrows with a Coke.

"Yeah, you're right, but I was at the brink of going to a higher level in my singing career."

"Look at what you already accomplished. Think about it, a few months ago you were a little girl with a big voice singing gospel music and living in a small town. Now you're a woman living in a big city as a working singer. It takes a lot of strength to leave your family and friends and start over in a new town. You are a force to be reckoned with my friend."

The phone rings.

"Hello."

"Hi Bobbi, it's your old friend Bishop Sam Collins."

"How in the hell did you get my number?"

"Is that how you talk to your manager and carrier of the Gospel?"

"You're my former manager and you're not worthy to be a Bishop."

"That's how I roll sweetheart."

"Yeah, I know how you roll, especially as a married man who sleeps with different women."

"You don't know anything about my private life, sweetheart, but I do know that you're still under contract as my client."

"You didn't do jack for my career. I'm the one who was booking my engagement while you were stepping out on your wife. So, I decided to expand my career beyond singing gospel."

"Young lady, I will take you to court if you don't honor our contract."

"I don't care about your stupid contract. To call me two months after I left Raycliffe shows how concern you are about my career. As I recall, you cared more about Miss Bonnie Stroud, someone whose body doesn't equal a pencil and can't carry a tune in a bucket. Not only were you giving her all the plum engagements, but you were also having an affair with her. I have the videos to prove it, so if you know what is good for you, you would abolish any ideas of taking me to court; if not, I would hate to hurt Miss. Rollins." The next sound I heard was the dial tone.

"Bobbi, was that Sam Collins you were speaking to?" Gretchen asks as she exercises in the living room.

"Yeah, that was him being a jerk."

"It sounds like you put him in his place."

"I regret that I was in a relationship with that scumbag."

"Now, we can put that scumbag behind us and move on."

"Talking about moving on, I got a hot date tonight with Hank Jackson."

"Is that the exercise instructor who flirted with you in the dance studio?"

"Yes, I can't wait to go out with him. That man is so handsome."

"Yeah, I got a performance tonight. I will be singing my usual songs."

The phone rings again.

"Okay, this phone is irritating me today."

"Hello."

"Hey Bobbi, its Aunt Katherine, Bishop Collins just called me and told me how rude you acted towards him. I'm very disappointed in the woman you're becoming. After all the things he has done for you, it is very unladylike for you to speak to him in a derogatory manner."

"I can't believe you're calling me and defending that sleaze bag. All he did was rip me off; he's continuing to rob from you and the rest of the congregation."

"The bible says give honor where honor is due."

"You're correct, but Bishop is not worthy of receiving honor from me. That man is nothing but a robber and a thief."

"I did not raise you that way, young lady."

"Aunt Katherine, you're deceiving yourself if you think Bishop Collins is honorable."

"My goodness, you are becoming more worldly and sassy just like your mother by the minute. When your mother got into the world, she started disrespecting authority, using profanity and hanging around all kinds of ungodly people. I bet you're still hanging around that scandalous white girl."

"You know what I think it's best if I hang up the phone now before I say something, I have no business saying."

I hung up the phone and place my head in my hands.

"Are you alright, Bobbi?" Gretchen asks me as her whole body is covered with sweat.

"That was my aunt taking up for Bishop Collins. Our friend called her and told her the conversation we had. I can't believe that man got my aunt snowed."

"Hey Bobbi, don't you remember that night a year ago when we danced the night away at Club Tinkerbelle."

"Yeah, I had to sneak out of the house to make it."

"I remember you sneaking out many nights so that you could have some fun."

I wonder what happened to the owner of Club Tinkerbelle, Mr. What His name."

"Are you talking about Mr. Stokes," Gretchen answers as she cools down from exercising.

"He and his wife retired, sold the club and moved to Florida. Their daughter, Molly, married an accountant and still lives in Raycliffe, and their son Michael is as gay as a three-dollar bill cross-dressing and living the party life in New York."

"Omg, I can't imagine Michael Stokes, who stands 6'4, weighing almost three hundred pounds wearing a dress," I said to Gretchen as we bawl in laughter.

"Please give it up for Miss. Bobbi Minor." The Master of Ceremonies announces as the crowd applauds.

I just finished performing my last set of the night at Club Clooney's. The owners need to call Home Depot and have them rebuild this club because I brought the house down tonight. The crowd usually goes nuts when I mesmerize them with my rendition of "This Bitter Earth." Things have been going pretty well since the Wanda Bash audition. Not only have I become a regular at Club Clooney's, but I've also gotten a small part in a stage play and I was chosen to perform the national anthem at a recent Falcon's football game. Things are also looking good for my Gretchen. She's now a backup dancer for Vanilla Ice, which causes her to be on the road for weeks. As I'm in the janitorial closet changing my outfit, I hear a knock on the door.

"Hi, my name is Donald Roman of Roman Enterprises. I would like to make you a star."

When I heard make you a star, I opened the door quickly. And when I opened the door, I saw this average height dude dressed in a two-piece black suit looking like Michael Douglas in a mafia film.

"Hey, come on into my lovely dressing room and tell me more about yourself," I said to him as I move some of the towels out the way.

"First and foremost, I must tell you, Miss Minor, you're one heck of a singer. I haven't heard a talent like you in decades. This is my third time watching you perform, and I am amazed."

"Tell me more about yourself?"

"I started in this business thirty years ago, working in the mailroom at a major record company. Then I became a touring manager for the Snooty Blues Band for six years. I created Donald Roman Enterprises because I was becoming frustrated with life on the road. Roman Enterprises enables me to manage other artists. I would love to help develop a talent like yours and make you a major force in this industry. Here's my card with my contact info. I love to work with you."

Wow, someone is interested in representing me. But I'm not going to get my hopes up. Bishop Collins is still fresh on my mind. I will do some research on Mr. Roman myself. I hope he can book me into venues with real dressing rooms.

When I got home from my performance, I told Gretchen about Mr. Roman and she immediately put me in contact with Entertainment Lawyer, Anthony Rosier. He looks at Mr. Roman's contract and confirms that he's legit. I found out that some of Mr. Roman's clients include the Snooty Blues Band, Sweet Betsy Blu, and Cannonball Paul. Due to being a hardcore jazz and blues fan, he's active in organizing festivals featuring acts from those genres. Once I sign the contract, he will book me at a casino in Biloxi, Mississippi. Mr. Roman's main goal is to help me get a recording deal. One of my musician friends, Rory Hill, took me to a recording studio near Chattahoochee Avenue a few weeks ago and produced a demo of me sing jazz and blues songs. Mr. Roman believes I can sing blues, jazz, standards, cabaret, and ballads. He even hired Madeline Braimwaite to be my vocal coach. Madeline is a formidable jazz vocalist in her own right.

I finally moved out of Techwood into an apartment on Piedmont Road overlooking Piedmont Park. I'm in it now unpacking while listening to an old Laura Lee record. Laura Lee, like myself, started in the church, then moved into the world of secular music. My Aunt Katherine who knew Laura in her gospel singing days, told me recently that she is now a minister. I'm so glad to be out of Techwood. As the church folks say, "Glory to God." This is a definite step up. It's a two-bedroom with a master bedroom, dishwasher, washer and dryer capabilities. The rent is $800 a month which is not bad at all for this area.

"Hey, Miss Superstar, how's life in your new apartment?" Gretchen asks as she walks in the living room looking as radiant as ever.

"I'm still trying to unpack my things, but once I'm finished, I will take a warm relaxing bath."

"I am so proud of you. You got a manager, a new home; soon, you will have a record deal. Now you need a man."

"You can set me up with Mr. Vanilla Ice. I love milk."

"Vanilla Ice is probably one of the last men you want to get with. He is such a sex hound."

"Oh….is there anything going on between you two?"

"No way, I like my black men. So, what you got lined up next?"

"I'm still performing at different venues working on getting to the next level." What have you been up to, Miss Gretchen?

"I am touring with the hot new recording duo Silk N Smooth as a dancer."

"Omg, they aren't anything but two pretty boys who can't sing to save their lives, but I wouldn't mind you set me up with one of them."

"Girl, I rather set you up with Don King than one of those wimps."

"Oh, they like that?"

"They both like saggy tacos."

"Saggy Tacos!" I laughingly state

"Yes, you don't want to get with no saggy tacos; you need a sizzling steak."

"All this talking about food is making me hungry, why don't I take you out to Longhorns to get some real steak.

Chapter Three

I'm a recording artist now. Two days ago, I signed a four-year contract with Climax Records, a small R&B label in Atlanta. Its proprietors Paul Haynes and Tim Gray, started the label in 1985. I talked to them briefly when they saw me perform at a nightclub in Washington, DC recently. Mr. Roman, Paul, Tim, and I were the only people present at the signing. The next day I went to the studio to record a jazz song called *When Love Goes Away*. It will be my first single that will be released next week. The next day I walked quietly into the studio recording booth and I happen to overhear a conversation between two of the studio engineers Ted Hanson and Bill Newton. These two guys have been giving me a hard time since I started recording my album.

"Yeah, that Bradley Dukes kid got a great career ahead of him," Ted says as he sweeps the floor with a broom.

"I can't wait to put the finishing touch on his album." Bill seriously states as he places chairs in various areas of the studio.

"I know one thing, I will be glad when we finish working with that black b****," Ted says with disdain.

"Oh yeah, that Bobbi gal thinks she's the tops, but she needs to be brought down a notch or two."

"This is not a place for those kinds of people."

Now these two guys were really pissing me off. Aunt Katherine used to tell me that ignorance has no power, but them referring me the way they're doing is bothering me.

"So, where is my place, gentleman?" I boldly asked with both hands on my hips.

"That is just like you people to listen in on other folks' conversation." Ted had the nerve to reply.

"Now, you two listen to me! I am a sexy full-figure black woman who will succeed regardless of your small-minded comments. Besides, it's you people that is diligently trying to emulate us by trying to take our music. So, if you don't like who I am, then you two know where you all can go."

"Now, listen to me you black whore!" Ted says to me as he forcefully grabs my neck.

"If you know what's good for you girl, you would shut your mouth."

"Get your hands off of her!" A familiar voice says.

It's my new friend Bradley Dukes coming to rescue me. He punched Ted in the face and he drops to the ground immediately. I immediately went to Bill and slapped the crap out of him.

"Don't you ever call any black b****! We are the queens of the earth!"

"You two bastards are fired, and I will make sure you two never work in this town again."

Bradley states.

"Are you okay?" Bradley asks as I prepare to leave the studio.

"I'm fine and thank you so much for defending me."

"No problem. Its 1992, I can't believe people are still

17

acting that way. I thank God my parents didn't raise me to live in bigotry and ignorance."

"Shoot, I'm hungry; where is a good restaurant around here that serves awesome food?"

"Sammy Joes Burgers Joint is the best." Why don't I treat you to lunch?

"That would be great."

Bradley and I had a great time at Sammy Joes, but I must've had powder on my face because some of the patrons looked at Bradley and me like some bloodhounds. Despite that, I had a good time. Bradley told me about his childhood in Arkansas and why he loves the blues. He showed me pictures of his wife and newborn daughter. I told him about my life growing up in Raycliffe and my excitement about my upcoming album.

When we went back to the studio, Tim called me into his office.

"Hey Bobbi, Paul and I decided to release the single *Highway to Rejection*. We think it's a good R&B song that will get you unto the mainstream."

"When are we going to finish recording my album?"

"We're not worried about an album our focus right now is to find you an audience with your singles. Once we get your audience, then we will proceed with recording an album."

"My first single has already gotten me an audience; it is always played on the radio. So, I don't think we need to prolong recording my album."

When Loves Goes Away was a successful debut single on the single jazz chart and placed on the Top 60 on the R&B charts which is not good."

"I still don't understand why I can't continue to record an album," I said as I began to become frustrated.

"Bobbi, I know it's frustrating now but I guarantee that if we get your sales up, we will record your album. In a few days, you're slated to be the opening act for Taste' the hit female group for Climax. You opening for them will bring you more espouser as an artist."

I really don't like working with other females, but I will go along to get through with the tour.

"Girl, you're giving us a run for our money out there."

"I can't fake it when I'm on stage; it's all about the heart and soul," I replied.

That's Sandra Duncan, the alto member of Taste.' The group consists of Sandra, Mona Latimore, and Sierra Leone. Paul Haynes discovered the ladies at a music conference a few months ago and signed them immediately. There first single *Lust at First Sight* is still in the Top Ten on both the Pop and R&B charts. I've been turning the stage out since I join their tour. Sandra and Mona are great chicks but Sierre Leone is something else. With her strong exotic African features, she thinks the world revolves around her. What she lacks in talents, she got in looks. I watched how she seduces the men in the audience with her charisma.

Sierre Leone abhors the thunderous standing ovation I receive after my performances and tonight is no exception.

"Girl, when you sing, your voice reminds me of being in the choir at church," Mona says in the dressing room that we all share. Then Sierre Leone made her diva-like entrance as she rolls her eyes.

"Bobbi was awesome, wasn't she Sierre Leone?" Sandra asks.

"Omg, she practically tore the roof off the place." Mona comments.

"Sandra and Mona, you two make sure you're on your mark tonight and don't you all dare make me look bad tonight." Sierre Leone warns arrogantly.

"Cow, don't make me cuss you out." Mona states

"Taste' consists of three women, not one," Sandra says as she prepares her makeup

"Well!" Sierre Leone exclaims and walks out of the dressing room.

At times like this, I'm glad I'm not part of a group. I remember as a child I and some of my childhood girlfriends use to organize ourselves as a singing group and enter talent shows but the other girls would get mad at me because my voice stood out from everybody else. I eventually had to fight with one of the girls in the group because she wanted all the attention. Miss Sierre Leone remind me of her. Despite her attitude, I read an article that's written about me in the latest issue of *Scale* magazine.

Star on the Rise by Marsha Tripoli

Bobbi Minor is an absolute vocal powerhouse. Presently she's the opening act of the Taste' tour. Many of the concert goers clearly see that when Ms. Minor opens her mouth, she should be the headlining act. Minor, a gospel trained vocalist, have been a recording artist with Climax Records for a few months. In that short period of time, she has made her mark in the Jazz scene. Her first single "When Love Goes Away" hit the top Ten on the Jazz singles chart. What sets her apart from any other jazz vocalist is the intense vocals that she ads to her performances.

Chapter Four

Wow, it's nice being in my home. For a week, all I've done is sleep and rest my vocals. I needed rest, especially after the tour with Taste.' Sierre Leone went to Paul and Tim and demanded that I be kicked off their tour. I was really cooking on stage because Paul came and told me that I was giving his act a hard time. But I can't be hung up on Sierre Leone and her insecurities. My single, *Highway to Rejection* hit #26 on the Rhythm and Blues charts and I'm going to be the opening act on the Bradley Dukes tour. The tour starts on Monday in Kalamazoo, Michigan. I am excited about touring with him. I also had to fire Mr.Troman; he wasn't doing much for me anyway. He didn't know what direction he wanted me to go. One minute I was performing at a jazz venue, the next minute I was performing at a blues festival. He was basically giving me a bunch of empty promises, such as appearing on *The Arsenio Hall Show* and the Montreux Jazz Festival. I want immediate results, not empty promises. Even though I have two hit singles, I still need to build my name as an artist. Also, I'm trying to get Climax to give me more mainstream songs.

My being fired from the Taste' tour, I must admit has brought me a lot of publicity due to me outshining the headliner. If I was constantly touring, I would be selling more records. I don't know why I haven't done a video for both of my singles. Then I hear the doorbell ring. I opened the door and I couldn't believe my eyes.

"What are you standing there for? Come give your parents a hug."

What in the world are my parents doing here? I haven't spoken to Howard and Deborah Minor in over a year. My mother, known to the world as Debbie Love, the famous R&B diva, stands before me wearing a green dress looking like a watermelon in heels. My father Howard Dean Minor is wearing a two-piece white suit looking like Boss Hoggs on the *Dukes of Hazard*.

"How did you guys find out where I live?"

"It's a shame I had to find out from your Aunt where my daughter lives." Deborah angrily states.

"It's a shame that I can never get a hold of my parents." I retort with a hint of sarcasm.

"Your Aunt Kat called me a month ago, proclaiming that you inherited the same demon from me to sing the devil music. She came across very crass and rude to me." Deborah says.

Indeed, I did inherit my singing ability from my mother's side of the family, starting with my late grandparents Bishop Daniel and Luttibelle Toombs, who pastored a small COGIC congregation in Griffin, Georgia for many years. Daniel possessed a strong roaring voice. Luttibelle could've given Mahalia Jackson a run for her money with her voice. Their five daughters Iola, Katherine, Deborah, Josephine and Lucinda, can sing. In fact, they formed a gospel singing group calling themselves the Toombs Sisters. They traveled throughout the South, singing at various churches where people would flock to hear them sing. Deborah had the strongest voice out of the five sisters,' and this made her sing lead. While touring, Deborah met a young gospel groupie named Howard Minor.

Howard was born in Mississippi, coming from a family of cooks and restaurant owners, made Howard have a strong business mind. In the late '60s, while performing in a storefront church in Jackson, Mississippi, Howard dark-skinned, stocky build weighing almost 300lbs became hypnotized by a svelte lead singer of a family gospel group. My mother always tells me that my father wasn't her type, but the way he carried himself attracted her to him. My parents pursued a long-distance relationship before it was in style. My father encouraged my mother to listen to Aretha Franklin and Gladys Knight. My grandfather reframed my mother and aunts from listening to secular music and was dismayed when my mother started neglecting her obligations to the group.

Right before a group engagement in South Carolina, my mother ran away and married my father at the age of nineteen. This brought the disbandment to the Toombs Sisters. My mother then began contemplating a career as a soul singer just like Aretha Franklin, who was burning up the charts in those days. My father had so much faith in my mother's ability to be a soul singer that he managed to get her booked into some nightclubs.

In the fall of 1972, some record executives came to one of my mother's performances and expressed interest in her, signing her to a recording deal with Hotmaster Records. She released her debut album, which climbed the top ten on the R&B album charts. She began traveling the chitlin circuit performing at venues across America that catered to the African American audience. While on tour, my mother realized that she was pregnant with me. When someone becomes a parent, that child supposed to be the priority. I've been priority number two in my parents' life for years. After I was born, my parents left me in the loving care of my Aunt Katherine, who then became the musical director at St. Paul COGIC, a position she holds till this day.

In 1975 my father believed that my mother could attract a larger audience by recording a new form of music called disco. My mother became one of the first artists to attain success in that genre. My parents traveled the world while I was stuck in the Raycliffe, GA living with an aunt in a strict religious environment. My parents would visit sporadically, but the closeness was not there and it remains that way till this day. Now my mother is in my house parading around like she's Cicely Tyson.

"I wish you told your father and me that you wanted to pursue a recording career. He can be your manager." Deborah sternly states. "The music biz is a lot different than it was in your heyday," I reply with my hands on my hips.

"But your father still has connection and if you allow him to help you sweetie you will be more successful in your career than you are now."

"I'm fine with doing session work besides; I want to make it on my own merits not based on my parents."

"Okay...Okay..." Deborah says with agitation. "Let's talk about this furniture my dear. I've taken up interior design in recent years and I can do wonders with this apartment."

She has the nerve talking about my apartment. I'm ready for them to leave.

"How long are you all supposed to be in town?" I ask in frustration. "Just for a few days, your mother is booked to perform at a Dance Extravaganza in Buckhead; I think the audience will be full of faggots."

"Now you watch your mouth Deanie Bug those faggots are my biggest fans! On that note, we got to head out for rehearsal!"

"We got to do lunch tomorrow honey!" Howard says as he and Deborah prepares to go to depart.

"Bye yawl."

Wow, that was an interesting visit. I need to rest before my performance tonight.

The Happy Corner, a hellhole bar on the corner of Buckhound Hwy and Douglass Road. This place is full of whores and pimps. I'm here for only one night and believe me; I will never return. Ever since I fired Mr. Troman, I started to book myself into small nightclubs. Some of the gigs I've attained for myself haven't' been glamorous. I'm standing at the bar waiting for my turn to go on stage. I decided to wear a blue and green sparkly gown that I bought at Lane Bryant. No manager, no new outfits, no promotions. In fact, Tim and Paul are putting all their energy into Taste.' They get all the publicity, major tour, major TV shows, and hit records. I recorded a song called *I Need a Good Man,* which was supposed to be my next single. A few days later, I turned on the radio and I heard the song on the radio; it didn't have my vocals but Taste's vocals. Tim and Paul has nothing to do with me unless they want me to come into the studio and record some background vocals or record songs that Taste' reject and release them as singles, which would climb on the lower tier of the R&B charts. My career has now resorted to performing in dumps like this.

"Does the house band know any of my songs?" I asked the manager of the club.

"Look babe, just get up there and do some Aretha or Chaka." He replied.

"Sing some Aretha or some Chaka," I exclaimed. "I have my songs; I don't need to sing theirs."

"Look lady, you either sing what the band knows, or you split." The manager says before he walked away.

"Since I needed the money, I told the leader of the house band to play *Dr. Feel-Good and Sweet Thing.*

Despite the house band lousiness, I manage to turn the Happy Corner out. I ended up doing three encores, but after I got my money, I left that place as fast as I could. I got home and checked out my answering machine and I hear this deep sexy baritone voice.

"Hi, my name is William Blair and I am a writer and director of the play *Sweet, Sweet Raspberry.* Please call me ASAP.

Omg! William Blair wants to talk to me.

Chapter Five

I'm at Brewster's Rapture a nice Coffee House in the Midtown Atlanta area. I'm here waiting to meet Mr. William Blair. The aroma of the freshly brewed coffee immediately engulfs me. Not only does the coffee smell awesome, but I'm blown away at how the place is decorated with teal blue walls with chocolate brown flooring. The furniture is very vintage and relaxing. I decide to take a seat by the window. I'm so excited to be meeting the great William Blair. It seems like every month; he produces a gospel stage play.

I saw a silver two-door Mercedes 500sl convertible drive into the parking lot. That got to be no one other than Mr. William Blair. It is only someone with his status that would drive a vehicle like that.

Stepping out the automobile is this tall six-foot figure with tight blue jeans and a black leather jacket. The skin on this gentleman radiates like a black stallion horse. William Blair is quite a vision of a dude. As he was walking towards the coffeehouse, I did a last-minute check on my hair and makeup. I recently dyed my hair honey blonde and the black dress I'm wearing makes me look like a performer from the 1930s. Before I knew it, he's standing before me with a megawatt smile.

"Hi Mr. Blair, I am so honored to meet you," I said as I stood up to give him a hug.

My goodness, he's hugging me tightly. It's been so long since I got hugged by a man—especially a man that is taller than me.

"I must say, you are one stunning woman." William compliments, making me blush like a rose garden.

"Thank you, sir." Is the only statement I'm able to make as I return to my seat.

"I can't believe I am sitting across from Bobbi Minor the best singer I've ever heard since Dinah Washington."

"Oh stop, your plays are absolutely the best thing going on in the theatre world right now."

"I hope you like it here at Brewster's."

"Mr. Blair this place is divine from the ambience to the coffee itself."

"Please call me William," William says smoothly as he takes my hand and starts to rub it.

"Okay, the reason I wanted to meet you is because I have you in mind for a part in my next stage play. I believe you have some acting talents that is waiting to be seen."

"Indeed, I want to pursue more acting, and I'm carefully looking over some projects right now."

"But look no more Bobbi. I have the part that is tailor-made for you." As William was speaking, I noticed how handsome he is. This made me question whether he's gay or not. I've been around gay men all my life, especially when I was on the gospel circuit. I was briefly involved with a gay Caucasian pianist name Bryan Lucas. He had light blond hair, the prettiest blue eyes, and a body that make Tom Cruise look like a milk carton. He always wore the latest fashions. I met Bryan when I was the opening performer for Vance "Thunderstorm" Johnson. Bryan was his accompanist. That boy could play gospel on a piano better than most black fellows I know. When he opened his mouth, I immediately knew he was gay. He told me he has always been fascinated with black gospel. As a scholarship student at Cincinnati Conservatory of Music, he began playing the piano at several local black churches. That's how he became part of Thunderstorms band.

Thunderstorm is a trip in half. He's known for his dynamic performances, his flamboyant mannerism and his outrageous outfits. This man usually turns a place out with his strong performances. He tried to get fresh with me and I rejected his advances. When he found out that I was involved with Bryan, I was kicked off the tour. I was seventeen and Bryan was twenty-six. Descending from an aristocratic family, he introduced me to the fine things of life. He would frequently take me to operas and ballets in the Atlanta area. Despite my weight, Bryan constantly told me how beautiful I was. Also, he gave me my first kiss. My God, that man can kiss. Aunt Kat being the godly woman that she is didn't like me dating a white man, but Bryan gave me the confidence and affirmation that no one else could give me.

Life struck me a mighty blow when Bryan contracted terminal cancer. Bryan went from looking like an angel to almost being unbearable for me to look at because the disease was eating him up badly. I was the only one who stood by him after everyone turned their back on him. He said he wanted to marry me, and I believe we would've been happy together. He even managed to come to my high school graduation when he knew he should've been resting. He died a few months later. I miss him dearly.

Now I'm sitting here in front of Mr. William Blair. I know one thing he sure can talk. He has been talking a mile a minute since we sat down. He gave me a copy of the script of the new play and I look it over. But the rest of our meeting was uneventful. My mind was still on Bryan.

It took me a month to decide to join the cast of *Don't Come Selling Me Wolf Tickets* even though I was done looking at the script in two days. William's production company will be producing the play in the spring. William Blair continues to call me, coming off very co-dependent. He's constantly whining about why I don't call him, and he gets angry when I'm not available. But I don't mind him taking me out though. But I'm not interested in getting serious with William right now. My focus is my career.

My recording career is still stuck in neutral. Paul or Tim hasn't contacted me in weeks. Recently the media has been having a field day concerning the romantic affair between Paul Hayes and that Sierre Leone person. The couple has been feature looking all lovey-dovey on every cover of any tabloid magazine that you can imagine. I feel that my career is suffering. When Paul and Tim first signed me to Climax Records, they had such admiration for me. They gave me a lot of promises about what they were going to do for me as an artist, but when Taste' was signed to the label, they became priority. I will never forget Paul coming to me after I was kicked off the Taste' tour laughingly telling me that I was giving his act a hard time. It's not my fault that Sierre Leon lacks vocal talent even though she's an excellent performer. I always put forth a lot of heart and soul in each of my performances. That's how I was raised, and that's how I maintain standards. Sierre Leon got glitter and glamour which will only go so far before it begins to decay. Soul will last a lifetime. It's the beginning of a new year and I am relaxing in my love seat until the doorbell rings.

"Who is it?" I asked

"It's Gretchen" The voice replied.

I opened the door and sure enough, it was my best friend Gretchen Fanning, who I haven't seen in months. The Gretchen I know used to wear the latest fashion but the girl that is standing in front of me is emaciated wearing a simple white T-shirt and black jogging pants. Her hair hasn't been combed and I can see several bruises on both of her arms.

"Girl, how have you been!?" Get in here and give me a hug. As we embrace, Gretchen breakdown in tears.

"What's the matter?" I ask Gretchen as I grab ahold of her hand and led her into the living so she could sit down on the sofa.

"Bobbi, I left Antonio," Gretchen states as she continues to bawl over in tears.

Shortly after I got my record deal, Gretchen became romantically involved with Antonio Sims, an upcoming hip-hop record producer. The more Gretchen got involved with Antonio, the more distant she became. She wouldn't return my calls at all. I sat next to her, trying to console her. Then she finally comports herself to speak.

"Well, the last time we saw each other, I had gotten involved with Antonio. When we first met, he treated me like a queen. Buying me flowers and writing me love notes every day. Then I moved in with him. After I moved in with

Antonio, that's when things started changing. He started to become possessive by constantly inquiring to know where I was or what I was doing. The only place he allowed me to go was the grocery store. He monitored who I kept contact with. He rarely allowed me to speak with my family and totally cut my friends out of my life. I wanted to call you so badly, but he would go ballistic when I would communicate with anyone else. Also, he started physically harming me and locking me in the closet for hours if I disobeyed him."

I'm totally shocked. I can't believe my friend went through this ordeal.

"So, what brought you here?" I asked as I wiped the tears from my face.

"I'm was in the house doing the laundry and he came in the house angry, angry that a rapper rejected one of the songs that he had written for them. So he wanted to take his anger out on me. At that point, I was already tired and frustrated with how he treated me, and I started to retaliate which infuriated him even more to the point where he tried to pure gas on me and set me on fire. I managed to grab my keys and wallet and break away from him."

"Wow, I am so glad you were able to break away from all of that craziness. You're blessed to be alive."

"I'm blessed to see you again. I missed you so much." Gretchen says as she smiles for the first time since she came over.

"I miss you too. Now you're not going back to that mess. Where are your bags?"

"All the cloths I got are the ones I'm wearing. Antonio can have my old clothing; they didn't represent who I am anyway."

"That right, we will get you new clothing. You can stay here and we will shop for new cloths."

"It's been so long since I went shopping for clothes." Antonio forcefully made me wear t-shirts and jogging pants.

"He must be running a gym." I sarcastically stated as I walk Gretchen to my guest room.

"He figures that sweatpants would draw less attention from other men."

"That dude was a pure fool in all caps," I comment.

"Bobbi you are so hilarious, but seriously I decided I'm going to throw out the old and bring in the new. Thank you so much Bobbi for allowing me to stay with you. I promise you I won't be here for long." Gretchen exclaims. "Now let's talk about you Miss Lady. For several months I've been watching you and reading about you in all the magazines. I even read that article in JET magazine about how you stole the show from that new girl group, Taste'. I've heard rumors that Sierre Leone had you kick off the tour."

"Yeah, that witch and I don't get along, in fact, she was the one who had me kicked off the tour because of the standing ovations I was receiving from the crowd."

"How's your love life missy?" Gretchen asks emphasizing the word love.

"Right now, I'm seeing this gentleman by the name of William Blair."

"William Blair, the playwright! Omg, what is he like!" Gretchen shouts, sounding like a high school cheerleader.

"I will be in his next play this summer."

"You've gone and caught you a find piece of chocolate. So how did you guys meet?"

"He called me leaving a message that he wants me to be a part of his play."

"How is he in bed?" Gretchen asked

"Gretchen?!"

"Come on. Do Tell! Do Tell!"

"Alright, the other night, he invited me to his house. I'm glad he did because I had a bad day due to an argument with the record company. So when I arrived, William was wearing this sexy silk red robe. I just needed him to hold me and tell me that everything's going to be okay. He did that and much more.

"What do you mean that and so much more?" Gretchen asked curiously.

"I'm not telling you sweetie. All I can say is that William knows his way around. But I think something ain't right about him though."

"Ooooo, here we go again." Gretchen sighs, shaking her head, knowing that I've been down this road before.

"I know Gretchen; I am always attracting brothers that are not stable.

CHAPTER SIX

I can't believe it. The receptionist at Climax Records left a message on my answer machine telling me I'm no longer a part of the company. I am officially without a record label. Not only I've been drop without being told a reason, both Paul and Tim did not have the common courtesy to tell me themselves which really hurt. I grabbed a glass and threw it against the wall.

"Bobbi Open Up! What' going on!" Gretchen screams as she bangs on my bedroom door. I opened the door and immediately started to sob as Gretchen held me in her arms.

"What's the matter?"

"The record company left a message on my answering machine telling me I'm no longer a part of it."

"What do you mean you're not a part of the company?"

"I've been drop. I will no longer be with Climax Records anymore as a recording artist."

"They can't do that to you. You signed a contract."

"I don't know but I'm furious that Paul and Tim had their secretary call and leave me a message instead of them telling me themselves."

"Bobbi do not worry about them; you need to contact a lawyer and see if Climax Records acted against the contract.

If not, another record company will be more than happy to sign you with them."

Gretchen is right; I do need to contact a lawyer and find out what my options are. I needed to get my mind off the matter, so I decided to turn the TV on. Mary J. Blige appears on the screen. Mary J. Blige came into the music scene last year and blazed the charts with her combination of hip-hop and soul.

"That girl reminds me so much of you," Gretchen comments as she stares at the TV.

"Yeah, she started in the church just like I did and we're around the same age. I would do anything to be in her shoes right now."

Gretchen then cuts the TV off. I guess she was cognoscente to the fact that I was getting sad by watching Mary J. Blige, whose career is soaring while mine is sinking.

"Bobbi, we need to get you some work ASAP. We got to keep your name out regardless of whether you have a record out or a record company behind you."

"I got bookings all the way up to the springtime.

William and I are growing closer and closer. He doesn't know my itinerary, but he manages to have red roses delivered to all of my performances. We can't keep our hands off of each other during rehearsal for *Don't Come Selling Me Wolf Tickets*. In the play, I portray a character name Versa, a strong-minded woman who caught her husband cheating with another woman. I hope that me doing this play will introduce myself to a new audience that never knew me. Also, I've been the opening act for Jazz Extreme, a new acid jazz band that is beginning to make some ranks in the music scene. The group manager saw one of my performances and immediately invited me to join their tour. The members of the band are an interesting group of people. Boris Wade, the founder of the group, is a serious-minded fellow who diligently keeps the other members straight. Boris plays bass; Michael Bridges, an Adonis blond looking guy from Wyoming, plays the electric guitar; Wade Tompkins, a Jim Belushi look-alike plays the drums; Baylor "Bay Bay" Kennedy started out as a child prodigy; and Karen Cho is an openly bisexual Asian woman who sings vocals. Wade can sometimes come off very eccentric due to his fascination with Batman. Michael can sometimes have the intelligence of a flat tire, but he can utilize his attractiveness to get his way. Bay, on the other hand, enjoys devouring pages of English Literature from the 1800's. Karen has a deep singing voice kind of reminiscent of Mavis Staples. This tour has afforded me the privilege to perform at college campuses, classier small jazz venues a step up from the establishments I'm usually booked in.

Tonight we have a gig at Humphrey College, a small all-girls' liberal arts college, in Decatur, GA. Gretchen is in the dressing room, helping me put on my outfit. I had thought about entering college to study music but didn't need some college professor telling me how to sing. I had enough of that coming from Aunt Kat when I was growing up.

"Have you spoken with your Aunt?" Gretchen asks me.

"I haven't' spoken with that woman since she got on me for going against Reverend Freak- A- Lot."

"You are hilarious."

"When was the last time you spoke with your family?" I asked Gretchen.

"I told my mother that I left Tony and she couldn't be

more thrilled. She wouldn't be any happier if I was to come home. My father is a different story."

"What's the issue with your father?"

"You know my father kicked me out when I was fifteen."

"You never told me the details as far as why your father kicked you out."

Gretchen sat down in the chair and began to share her story.

"When I was fifteen, I got involved with a man named Blake. Blake was 25 and was a manager at a local bank. We both knew it was wrong to be with each other, but you can't knock down the hand of love when it comes your way. Blake and I were head over heels in love. He was very romantic. Every time we see each other, he would always present me with a gift, from a bouquet of red roses to chocolate candy. Blake wanted to marry me and was willing to wait until I became of age. We were very discreet about our relationship, but my father thought I was being promiscuous with other men. So I started rebelling. I started skipping school and coming home late. Everything came to a head when I came home past my curfew. The moment I walked into the house, my father started yelling at me about coming home late. My father was always stern and verbally abusive towards me. So, father and I started arguing back and forth until finally, my father slapped me real hard, called me a slut and demanded that I leave his house. I did just that and I haven't seen or spoken with my father since then."

"What happened between you and Blake?"

"I moved in with him and things were going really well for a few years before he started being abusive. So I endure his abuse until high school graduation night when I packed my things and headed here in Atlanta, I haven't looked back since then.

"Wow... I didn't know you were going through all of that."

"Omg, you're still here?!" Karen yells in her strong Chinese accent at Gretchen as she comes into my dressing room.

"It would be appropriate if you knock before you come barging into somewhere you're not wanted," Gretchen says as she stands up and walks towards Karen.

"Why don't you go and find a John to service!"

"Why don't you go and kill another cat and eat it!" Gretchen yells as she and Karen came face to face with each other.

"Both of yawl stop!" I yelled as I come between the two ladies defusing a brawl. These two don't get along like oil and water.

"You go on stage in five minutes Miss Minor!" The stage manager yells.

"Okay, you go out there and break a leg." Gretchen encouragingly said to me as she leaves the dressing room.

The concert was awesome. Those female students were acting like released prison inmates, the way they were flocking to the boys in Extreme. Even Karen was using Humphrey College as a meat marker to get girls. My focus is to sing my songs, get my check and go home. Wham, Bam, Thank you Ma'am. Now it's dark outside. The members of Extreme decided to stay for an after-party. I'm not one of those people who have to constantly party, so I decided to walk to the train station and take the train home. As I was walking, I realized how affluent this side of Decatur is in comparison to the South part of the city. Nice manicured yards, trendy little shops, restaurants that make New York-style pizzas. I have to come back here when I'm not busy. My mission now is to get home and lay my body down. Guess who's at the street corner? That old Mr. Hellmann doing what he does best. I continued walking. That man is something else.

I heard this loud noise once I've walked further away from the college, but I can't pinpoint where the sound was coming from. A flood of fear engulfs me and I realized that if I don't get to the train station that something crazy may happen.

"Hey, fat girl, why don't you take a stroll along the alley with me?!" A man with a strong masculine baritone voice yells. Then suddenly, I'm forcefully taken along this back alley behind the elderly home.

"If you scream one time, I will kill you. Just do what I tell you and you will be just fine." The predator states.

I can't see who this person is because he's covered in all-black attire. I'm behind this nursing home with my life in jeopardy and in total shock.

"Yeah, I got you right where I wantcha, you fat black whore." The person says in a psychotic slow kind of way.

"Please don't kill me," I say fearfully, with tears streaming down my face.

The man then slaps me across my face so hard.

"Don't you say another damn word, you fat piece of crap!"

I couldn't believe what was happening to me.

"What I'm going to have you do next is going to be

enjoyable for both of us." The man says to me as he unzips his pants.

"All you black whores are good for one thing," he continues to say before revealing his penis.

"You're going to get on your knees and take care of my instrument, you fat black whore. You're going to really enjoy making me feel good."

The fear that I had in me was now turning into anger. I'm assuming this sick moron is white because of the disparaging words that are coming out from his mouth. I'm going to make him feel good, alright.

"Oh yes, I love to make you feel good sir." I mockingly say to the man. I grab his instrument and twist it as if I'm twisting the water off a wet rag.

"Do you feel good now, you sick bastard?!" "Do you feel really good?!"

"I'm not a black whore; I'm a strong black woman!" "Do you hear me?!" "Woman!" "W.O.M.A.N!"

The jerk is now screaming his head off.

"Take that hood off your head!"

"He takes it off and the man is a red-head dude who resembles Ron Howard during his years on Happy Days.

"Tell me your name!"

"Harper Wintinbagel!" He barely said as I continued to twist his organ.

"Well, Harper, this whole city is getting ready to find out how sick of a moron you are disrespecting black sisters like me.

Still holding Harper's instrument, I walked out from

behind the nursing home and started telling every person I see what Harper did to me.

"This psycho tried to make me do sexual acts on him!" I yelled to the public until I was able to flag down the police.

"Ma'am what on earth is going on here?!" The officer asks.

"This damn bastard took me against my will behind the nursing home and tried to force me to do sexual favors for him."

"Miss let the man go." I let go and Harper falls to the ground into a fetal position.

"You will think twice about trying to get a black sister to make you feel good."

"Miss Minor, I think you caught a suspect that has been going around sexually assaulting young college women." The officer tells me as he places hand cups on Harper and placed him in the police vehicle.

"Ma'am I'm going to need you to come with me to the police station to make a statement.

Chapter Seven

I called Gretchen and the members of Extreme immediately after I made a statement at the police station. Ten minutes later, all of them showed up at the station to check if I'm okay. While at the station, Karen tells me that her stepfather molested her on several occasions when she was a teenager and when she told her mother what happened, she didn't believe her. Being at the police station is not fun. You see all kinds of weird folks being placed in jail. Gretchen eventually drives me home and I will never forget the concern everyone had for me.

I'm still trying to get a record deal. I'm totally bored waiting on the phone to ring for job opportunities. I still have no management, no agent, nothing. So, I must depend on myself to get work again. Hip Hop music is taking over the airwaves and I can't seem to get a break anywhere. Occasionally I get the gigs at these funky down cheap dives where I'm singing all over the musical map. Blues one night, Jazz another, and R&B the next night.

Jazz purists really don't take me seriously because of my gospel infused vocals. Blues enthusiast doesn't take me seriously because in their opinion I haven't experienced enough hurt and pain in order to sing blues. I lay on my sofa, trying to relax listening to Dusty Springfield *In Memphis* album before Gretchen comes barging in.

"Hey girl," Gretchen says as she cuts my radio off like she owns it.

"I want you to meet somebody."

"Chile, I'm trying to rest; I ain't in the mood to be bothered with nobody."

"He's outside waiting to meet you, go hurry and put something on."

Oh no, she didn't just roll up in my house and tell me to put something on. But I'm curious of who she brought to meet me, so I put on my sweatpants and a t-shirt and comb my hair into a ponytail.

"Bobbi, I want you to meet Gene Thomas, he's a talent manager who has been getting me dancing jobs."

Who is this clown that Gretchen brought in my house? This dude looks like he has an eating disorder. The suit he's wearing looks like it's about to swallow him.

"Nice to meet you Mr. Thomas."

"I just had to have you two meets. When I told Gene that I knew you, he immediately wanted me to introduce you to him." Gretchen excitingly says holding Gene's arm.

"I just love your voice. I hate that your record company didn't see how valuable you are as a singer. I would love to help make you the superstar that you deserve to be." Gene says in his Inspector Gadget like voice.

"I tell you what Mr. Thomas, why don't you go to the kitchen and fix yourself a drink while I speak to my friend for a minute.

"Come with me," I told Gretchen as we walked to my

bedroom. Once we entered my bedroom, I let Gretchen have it.

"Why did you bring that man over here? He's not going to do anything for me looking like an extra from the Dick Tracy movie."

"Bobbi, he's a good guy and I believe he can take your career to the next level."

"Gretchen first impressions are very important to me. If a person is sloppy in their dress, that person will be sloppy in how they handle their business dealings. Therefore, I will not be using his services."

"But Bobbi, Gene Thomas can help you get far ahead besides he's getting me jobs dancing for some of the best artists in the industry today."

"He may be good for you, but I have a feeling that he's not good for me."

"Okay, it's your call," Gretchen says as she exits my bedroom.

I'm very selective now of whom I want to handle my career. Just because they say I want to make you a superstar doesn't mean they can make you one—the phone rings.

"Hello"

"Hi, Bobbi this is William, do you have time to talk."

"I miss you so much; I just had to see you," Williams says as he sits across me.

"I've been so busy with my plays that I haven't had time to give a call. So, what have you been up to?"

I know this man isn't holding my hand as we sit across from each other at Austin's, one of the exclusive premiere restaurants in Atlanta. William had called me last night after weeks of not speaking to me. He got pissed off at me for dropping out of *Sweet, Sweet, Raspberry*. This man cursed me out when I told him I want to concentrate more on my music career. Now he's talking to me like I'm his lost love. He got to do a lot more to get back into my good graces.

"Well, I'm sure you know that my record company dropped me from their roster but I'm still working steadily doing live shows.

"You see, that's the reason you should've remained in the play." William sarcastically states.

"William, don't go there with me. You knew I was an established artist before you cast me in that play."

"It seems like you are no longer established now."

"Look, why don't you take that diva acting attitude somewhere else. I've never been around someone as selfish as you."

"You're the one who is selfish. I needed you to do the extended dates for the play, but no, you had to concentrate on yourself!"

"I had honored my commitments to do your play; therefore, I wasn't obligated to be in your damn play beyond what was stated in my contract. On that note, I will step away from your presence."

I collected my purse and left him. I can't believe I wasted time with that selfish bastard. He thinks I'm supposed to put my life on hold to do his plays. I think that's one of the problems that women have when they get involved with a man; they lose who they are. Men can be so selfish at times. I left the restaurant, and now I must erase him out of my mind.

Chapter Eight

This tour is so boring. I'm tired of singing the same songs repeatedly. Beulah Mae Clemmons, the legendary blues singer, is my boss now. I've been singing background for her for the last five months. I've performed with Beulah at every Blues Festival you can imagine. Beulah has given me opportunities to perform solo as the opening act a couple of times, but when she noticed the enormous response from the audience, those opportunities became sparse. Even her manager wanted to sign me and market me as a blues singer, but I refused right then and there. I don't want to go through that route again.

Today we are in Mobile, Alabama, for a couple of shows. I'm in my hotel room writing some songs due to Gretchen's urging me to do so.

"Girl, put that notebook down and go to the club with me." Mary McDaniel says as she gets ready to go out to the nightlife.

Mary is a white singer who sings background with me. Vocally she sounds like a black woman.

"Mary quit asking that girl to go out with you. Everybody is not into club life." Says Roema Coleman.

Roema is the other singer who sings backup with me

and Mary. Roema has been touring with Beulah for almost a year. In fact, she's a veteran in the music scene starting her career off in the seventies as the lead vocalist of the group Crème of Funk. They were the first call background group by the studio producers during the disco craze. My mother had them on her albums during that time. Crème of Funk even released a couple of disco albums of their own. Their biggest hit was *Sweet Funk* which climbed the on top five R&B and top twenty Pop charts. Roema left the group in 1980 to pursue a solo career. She has released several albums on her own but remained a force in the background world. In my opinion, I think Roema can sing circles around Beulah. Her singing will have you jumping out of your seat.

"Roema," Mary says "Bobbi needs to get out and live a little. All she does is sit in her room writing songs."

"Leave me alone; you need to stop going out so much, that's the reason you are tired so much when we are performing."

"Bobbi's right, lack of rest will ruin your ability to sing correctly. Roema concurred.

"Beulah doesn't have a problem with me; her problem is with Bobbi. She is always telling her she got a big body and her voice is too big."

Yeah, she got a point there. Beulah is constantly throwing insults my way.

Mary, Roema, and I are on stage at Mock Jock, a small blues joints in Huntsville, Alabama. This place is not different from the other blues venues where the conditions are deplorable—no mirrors in the dressing rooms, toilet overflowing, nowhere to dress and bad lighting. The music is starting. Beulah Mae, who is wearing a simple black dress, enters the stage and begins belting out "Motel Six Blues." We the background singers starts to harmonize behind her.

"Stop the music." Beulah Mae abruptly shouts."Bobbi, I told you to stop singing loud on my songs?"

I know this woman isn't trying to act ethnic towards me on stage at a live performance.

"I know you're not talking to me like that." I talked back with an attitude.

"Don't talk back to me. Remember, I'm your boss."

"You gonna go from boss lady to knock out lady if you don't watch your tone."

"Get your fat butt of my stage, before I throw you off," Beulah says as she approaches me and gets into my face.

Before I knew it, I gave Beulah Mae a right hook to the face. Two of her band members had to get me off of her. Beulah Mae did me a favor. She has a bad attitude. Like Aunt Kat used to tell me when I was growing up that you reap what you sow. So now, I'm heading to my hotel to get my things and split.

"Hey, Bobbi!!" Wait up!" Mary yells as she and Roema runs towards me.

"Immediately after you walked off the stage, Beulah Mae started saying mean things to me and Roema."

"How she treated you just now is very disrespectful. I'm going back to Virginia to focus on my family and directing the church choir." Roema says as she tries to catch her breath.

"Let's go get us something to eat and celebrate our newfound freedom," Mary suggests.

"Amen." Roema exclaims.

"How long you've known Beulah Mae?" I asked Roema as I chew down my hamburger and French Fries.

"I met her back in 1984 when she was recording, *I'm a Bad Mamma Jamma* album and we've had a professional relationship on and off since then. Most people think we are the best girlfriends, but we're not. The bible says I must be in the world but not of the world."

"So, you're quitting the music business?" Mary asks Roema.

"No, I'm going to record a gospel album. I want to go back to singing the songs I used to sing as a little girl. I miss those days of traveling all around the country with my family gospel singing group, praising God through song. The greatest benefit of singing gospel music is touching people and seeing their lives change."

As Roema was reminiscing about her gospel singing days, I start to think about my days as a gospel vocalist. The numerous times I didn't get paid and the bad accommodations that I lived in that sucked. Also, Roema didn't attain the solo superstardom that she deserves, so I think that's the reason why she's going back home.

"Well, I was going to share good news with you guys after the show, but I guess this is the best time to share." Mary says cheerfully but hesitant.

"Go on chile and spill it." Roema states.

"I just signed a recording deal with Jump Records a hip-hop label owned by MC Addiction. They want to make me the next Teena Marie."

"Girl congratulations." I hope she doesn't encounter the same problems I had with Climax Records.

"So, what are you going to do next, Bobbi?" Roema asks.

"I don't know what I'm going to do next."

"Baby girl, you know who holds tomorrow, Roema says as she holds my hand. She's getting on my nerves talking about God.

"I am full as the dickens," Mary says in a Southern drawl.

"Yeah, you ate your food like a starving fish." Roema laughingly comments.

"That comes from not eating anything all day."

"We need to go and pack our things and go home," I said.

"This is the last time we're going to be together," Mary says, being all sentimental.

"I'm going to miss you babies, but I'm not going to miss this business. Sometimes it will swallow you up and spit you out." Roema comments. I'm glad she didn't start talking about the church.

Together we walked out of the restaurant and back to the hotel. Mary is hopping on a plane to New York to record her first album, Roema is going back to her church choir. I'm back to nowhere.

Where in the world is that noise coming from? I just can't get any kind of rest. I put on my rod and walked down the hallway. As I got closer to my living room, it seems like a man and woman were arguing. I looked outside my living room window and I saw Gretchen and her ex-boyfriend Antonio arguing by the dumpster. I got to go and protect my friend. I dash out of my apartment and down the stairs like speedy Gonzalez.

"Don't yall realize that the whole neighborhood is fully awake because of all this screaming yall doing!" I yelled standing in front of Tony.

"Why don't you mind your business and take your Donkey Kong butt somewhere!" Antonio yells back.

"Who are you talking to you, pathetic excuse of a man?!"

"If I were you, I would go back to my apartment. You don't know what I'm capable of! Antonio yells, revealing all his gold teeth. This scumbag is really beginning to tick me off. Before I knew it, a force at the speed of a bullet landed on my face producing pains that I never felt before.

"I said, take your ass back into the apartment!" Antonio tells me. I cannot believe this man just slapped me.

"Don't hit my friend!" Gretchen says as she comes to me and holds my arm. I am astonished at what is transpiring. I'm getting angrier by the second.

Wham. I punch Antonio dead in his lip. All the rage and anger I have caused me to give Antonio the beating he will never forget. Then I picked Tony up like a WWF wrestler and threw him in the dumpster.

"I can't believe you just did that!" Gretchen says to me all hysterical.

I confidently told her "every week I throw the trash out." I'm appalled at the fact that Gretchen chose to associate herself with that bastard. I know one thing, all that fighting has made me hungry. I think I will exquisitely cook some strawberry pancakes for myself, the kind that Aunt Kat taught me. Or I might fix my famous shrimps and grits. As soon as I entered my apartment, the telephone rings.

"Hello."

"Bobbi, this is William."

"Hi William, how are you doing?" I say in my fake Carol Brady voice. I haven't heard from him in months.

"I will be in Atlanta this afternoon and I want to treat you to lunch, will you be available." This dude sounds like he's doing a toothpaste commercial. I have quite a busy schedule ahead of me today. But when I'm free, I will let you know."

"Okay, Bobbi. I understand. I would love to spend time with you."

After hanging up, the phone tears start flowing down my cheeks. Oh man, why do I love that man so much even to the point that I have to lie to him about my schedule? I just don't want to see that man after the way he has treated me in the past. Now he calls me as if nothing happened. I love him, but he's as fake as hell. Then I hear my door slam.

"Why in the hell did you throw Antonio in the dumpster like that?!" Gretchen shouts at me, looking like she been hit by a tornado.

"I know you're not yelling at me about that sorry man!"

"Bobbi, I still love him, and you had no right to beat him up that way."

"He had no right putting his hands on me that way, and what is wrong with you that you would allow yourself to become a punching bag."

"We still love each other and I'm going back to him."

"Hey, it's your life. I would rather die alone than be with someone who treats me like crap." I say to my friend as I went to the kitchen.

If Gretchen wants to be stupid and go with a man that is abusive than that's her prerogative, I'm not going to waste my energy on someone who wants to live in a mess. I got enough problems. I turn on my boom box and somehow Vanessa Bell Armstrong version of *Peace Be Still* appear. This song brings back so many memories. When that song first came out, Aunt Kat immediately had me sing in church with the choir. Growing up Vanessa Bell and Twinkie Clark of the famous Clark Sisters were the singers I vocally aspired to be like. I remember the rehearsals that I had with Aunt Kat, where she would throw the hymn book at me if I didn't hit a note the way she wanted me to hit it. I can hear Aunt Kat stern voice going in my head. "You sing it this way!!" Push it!!" Young lady, you're not singing loud enough." I better turn this radio off.

"Thanks for holding. Can I help you." Mr. Neloms is in a meeting right now, can I take a message." "I will make sure he gets it. Have a great day."

My goodness, that phone been ringing off the hook all morning long here at Thompson/Hopkins Associates. I never thought that I would have to do a regular job. A week after New Year's Day, I decided to apply for a job since my money was running low. I couldn't even attain session work. I was walking down Peachtree Street and saw a Help Wanted sign on the door of Thompson/Hopkins Associates, one of the biggest law firms in Atlanta. I went in and inquired about the sign and here I am, working as a receptionist. My co-workers don't know about my life as a recording artist. I go by the alias of Olivia Hines. As Olivia Hines, I work from 8am to 5pm Monday through Friday, basically answering phones. As Olivia Hines, I'm paid 12 dollars every hour with an hour lunch break. After 5pm, I go back to my normal life as Bobbi Minor, a struggling singer who once had the brass ring to be a famous star. After work today, I'm having dinner with William, so I can't wait for this day to be over.

I continued my normal routine answering phones, organizing appointments and then Paul Haynes and Sierra Leone walk in arm and arm. They are the last people I want to see. I wouldn't be in this present situation I'm in now if it wasn't for them. Now, here they come as if they rule the world.

"Hi, I'm Paul Haynes and I have an 11:30 appointment with Mr. Bruce Lucy".

"I will tell him you're here."

As I page Bruce Lucy, an associate attorney, Paul and Sierre Leone sit in the lobby. Sierre Leone is staring at me intensely. I'm trying my best to be oblivious of them both.

"Excuse me ma'am what's your name?" She asks me.

"Olivia Hines."

"You look like someone I used to work with."

"Yeah, you look very familiar to me as well." Paul comments. "You look like a singer that was signed to my label."

"I wish I could sing." I stated nervously as I shuffle papers around. Bruce Lucy arrives just in time to take Paul and Sierre Leone to his office. Wow, that was a close call. I guess today is my last day here.

CHAPTER NINE

I'm totally elated right now. William hasn't stop touching me since we met for dinner, and I love the way he touches me. As I'm sitting across from him at the table, I'm in total bliss.

"William, this is a lovely restaurant."

"The owner is a good friend of mines."

"Well, tell your friend what a great establishment he has. The ambiance, the lovely candles, the paintings on the walls and the food is scrumptious.

"I'm glad you're enjoying yourself. Let's talk about you. How's your singing career coming along?"

"It's not thriving like it was a year ago, but I'm moving along. In fact, I have a two-night engagement at the Purple Kitty in a few weeks." "The Purple Kitty?! That's one of the lousiest dives in the metro area."

"Hey, I got to pay the bills I can't go back to be a receptionist."

"I wish I saw you as a receptionist. That would've been hilarious."

"I did my job very well for that one week; I just couldn't work there and see famous people come in as clients of the firm."

"You realize that you don't belong in that kind of environment behind the desk but on stage," William says as he takes a bite off his salad. My God, this man good looking.

"Hello Bobbi," "Back to earth."

"I'm sorry, I guess I was daydreaming."

"Daydreaming about me sweetheart."

The way he said that statement just sent me through a windmill. I can't even contain myself. "You know what William, it's getting late and I must head home. I got a busy day tomorrow."

"I was hoping that we would go back to my place," William says as he comes over and gives me a nice kiss which takes total possession of me. I immediately collected my purse and walked arm and arm out the restaurant with William.

We got to William's place and we immediately begin to kiss each other passionately. Help me sweet Jesus; this man knows how to kiss. He led me to his bedroom. Like Wanda from Living Color said "I' ma Rock Your World. Williams has certainly rocked mine.

The Purple Kitty is a wasteland. The Kitty almost look like a pile of vomit. The best thing about this club is the purple cushy chairs with the kitty shape backside. Tonight is my last night here. I'm sitting in my dressing room waiting to go on stage.

"You will be going on in five minutes Miss Minor!" The manager yells.

I went to the mirror to do a final checkup on myself. The owner of the club requested that I wear something purple, so I decided to go retro with the fifties purple umbrella bottom like dress with white polka dots. Even my hairstyle is reminiscent of that era.

"Ladies and gentlemen put your hands together for recording star Bobbi Minor"! The house band immediately begins playing as I walk to the stage. Once I got behind the mic, I signaled the band to stop.

"Thank you for coming here tonight. I'm going to open my show with one of my favorite standards Embraceable You, everyone from Ella Fitzgerald to Frank Sinatra recorded this classic tune. I hope you enjoy it."

The crowd applause. Then I started my show. I performed for an hour singing jazz standards and received a standing ovation at the completion of my concert. There's nothing more gratifying than having the audience enjoy a performance. After I finished talking with some of the audience, I saw a familiar face standing before me. I'm surprised that Clarence Whitmore is here. I haven't seen him in a while. I still remember the date we went on and I must say he's looking hot.

"Hello stranger how are you doing?"

I'm doing great; just stop by to hear you sing."

"I don't recall ever telling you I was a performer."

"I knew who you were already, and I must say Bobbi, you are phenomenal." Clarence then took my hand and kissed it, sending a tingling sensation all over my body.

"Well, thank you Mr. Whitmore."

"Listen, I would love to take you out again."

"Okay sure, just give a girl a call, okay?"

"I'll hold you to that. I'll see you later." As Clarence left, I'm thinking in my mind how strange it is to show up to see me after months of no contact. I'm not attracted to Clarence like I am with William, but I am open to going out with Mr. Whitmore. I can't put all my eggs in one basket.

I got home from my performance and there's a party going on. Hip hop music is blasting in my house. What the hell is going on here? I specifically told Clarence not to have people in my house when I'm not present. A month after seeing Clarence at the Purple Kitty, I invited Clarence Whitmore to move in with me. William is acting flaky again. When I first met Clarence, he told me he does sales, but I realized recently that he sells drugs. He is dressing up in two-piece suits pretending to be going to an office where he works. I'm walking through my house in the midst of people I never met before in my life. When I walked into the living room, I saw mounds of drugs on the coffee table in a large bowl. That's it. This has gone on too far. I immediately started looking for Clarence. As I approached my bedroom, I hear some panting and moaning going on. I barged in and saw Clarence naked on top of a female in my bed.

"What in the hell is going on here!?" I screamed as I went further and drag Clarence off my bed.

"If you know what's good for you, you would get the hell out of here!" I yelled at the female. She quickly does what she's instructed "Baby, I love you; she doesn't mean anything to me," Clarence says to me as he scrambles to put his clothes on.

"I just don't mean anything to you if you are willing to bring a whore in my house and have sex with her on my bed. Not only that, but you also have all these damn people in my house with drugs on the living room table."

"Bobbi, I know I did wrong, but please forgive me."

This man must be crazy to think I'm going to do such a thing.

"Get your things and get the hell out of my house and get the hell out of my life!" I screamed as I walk out of my room to end the party.

"This party is over! Get the f*** out!!" The attendees went out of the house like roaches. How could I be this stupid and allow a man to move into my house and do this to me?

"Bobbi, please let work this out." Clarence pleads. I want to give him an Oscar for his fine performance right now.

"The only thing you worked on is my last nerve. Now get out."

Clarence suddenly turned on me like the devil has possessed his soul.

"I had that other woman here because I get tired of your fat a**. I like my women to be sexy. You aren't nothing but a frustrated fat b****." I slapped the hell out of him that he fell to the ground. This man got it confused if he thinks I'm going to let him get away with disrespecting me. Clarence stood up and dragged his sorry ass out. Now I got to clean this messy house.

CHAPTER TEN

"Wow, you sound good singing that song; you should record it." Bradley Dukes says to me as we talk to his dressing room. Bradley and his beautiful wife Clara are the few friends I have in show business. Bradley is appearing at the Ole Dixie House in Decatur, GA. I had to stop by to see him.

"I wish I could Brad but you know I don't have a record deal."

I'll see what I can do about that. Promise me that you'll never work a regular job again."

"Yeah I never thought my life would resort to working a regular job, but it made me realize how much I love show business."

I'm grateful for Bradley Dukes, when I was working I heard country singer Rochelle Leland singing *Hypnotized by Your Love* on the radio.

Once I heard it, I knew I had to record and release it as my next single but I'm not sure how I'm going to record it. When I got home from work, I called Bradley right away and sung the song to him. I got the love of country music for my country gospel singing Aunt Lucinda; there's a genuine simplicity in country music compared to R&B. I hear a knock on the door. It's William, I haven't seen him in weeks since we had that wonderful dinner date, but we spoke over the phone. Now he's here in the flesh.

"Why didn't you return my call?!"

"Well hello to you too."

"Answer my question!" William says with aggression as if he's my husband.

"I was busy!"

"When I call you, I expect you to return my calls." Now he beginning to make me nervous as he steps towards me and gets in my face.

"First of all, I don't have to do anything because I don't recall you changing my last name, second you need to watch how you address me."

I can't believe the William Blair encounter. I'm about to show him a side he has never seen before

"If you don't take your bipolar acting self out of my house, I will show you a side of me you've never seen before."

Then this man raises his hand and slaps me.

"Don't you ever talk to me that way you fat cow."

He's in it for now, I punched him in the face so hard you would have thought I was Mike Tyson.

"This is the last time I'm telling you to stay the hell out of my house, you have crossed the line big time."

I can't believe what just happened, that's not the William I fell in love with and I don't want him close to me.

I'm in Nashville in a recording studio preparing to record *Hypnotized by Your Love*. I'm excited to be back where I belong. It took me two days just to get be here. A month after my conversation with Bradley, he came to town on his tour and brought along Greg McVeigh of Highlight Records and introduced me to him. I performed the song for Greg and he immediately signed me to a one album deal right on the spot. Right now, I stand in the recording booth waiting on the recording engineer.

"Okay, Bobbi we're ready to go." The music starts and I began adding my vocals to the track. As I recorded the song, I thought of how William had me hypnotized by the way he treated me. The album contains some R&B and pop songs, this album is a total departure from the records I did at Climax. I look at the control booth and see Greg beaming. I will choose the songs that I can pour my heart into. Songs that I can relate to. Not songs that someone else chose for me.

"Hey, Bobbi I heard that you want to change your name?' Greg asks.

"Yes, I sure do. I no longer want to be Bobbi Minor, there's nothing minor about me and my talent. Barbara Rose Minor is my full name. But from now on I will call myself Barbrah Rose. Barbara spelled b a r b r a h. I don't need three A's.

"That's an awesome name." Greg and Bradley said.

"I'm going to release this song tomorrow to a couple of radio stations and take it from there so be on the lookout," Greg says.

I sure will. Clara, Bradley's wife, walks in with a plate of food and puts it in front of me, just in time. Bradley and Clara have really been taking care of me since I came to Nashville.

"Thank you so much Bradley for your faith in me. I

thought my career was over, but you, Greg and Clara came to my rescue. Clara, you need to give me the recipe to this peach cobbler."

The recipe is a family secret" Clara comments.

"Don't do me like that Clara," I said to her as I help her clean up.

All of a sudden Bradley frantically calls me into the living room. When I came to the living room, I saw the television news anchorwoman saying that William Blair is dead. I see the clip of William's body covered with a white sheet being carried on a stretcher in front of the hotel. Police said that Mr. Blair fell from the 15th floor of the hotel room to the ground ending his life. It was further reported that his body will be taken back to his hometown Milwaukee, where there will be a private burial.

"Hey, was William Blair the guy that you were dating" I couldn't hear Bradley at all. Seems like my heart stopped, despite what happened between Williams and me my love for him never changed but at the same time I knew I couldn't have a romantic relationship with him any longer; now he's gone. It seems apparent that Williams committed suicide. I realized that Bradley comforting me as I ball over in tears.

"Is she okay, Clara asks her husband and she hands me a Kleenex from the coffee table."

"I'm fine, I will get through this," I said to the both of them.

Greg McVeigh stood by his word after I recorded my first album, he released my version of *Hypnotize By Your*

Love it's a crossover hit, something that has been eluding me my entire career not only did the single climb number one R&B charts it climbed number 7 on the pop charts. I performed at the historic Apollo Theatre. I chose not to attend William's funeral because I want to remember the good times we had. Reports are coming out saying that he had schizophrenia. He will always hold a special place in my heart. I also signed with Thompson Hopkins as a client, they were shock when they found out who I was, and Alex Kayden is a manager Greg introduced me. I'm sitting across him now in his office in Nashville.

"Hello Miss Rose, how are you doing? Alex asks.

"I'm doing great."

I have several engagements lined up for you including the Essence Music Festival and extended tour in London. I'm still working on getting you in Vegas as well. Londoners have a strong affinity for black performers. Also, I want you to have more of a sexy image, in this day and age image has to match your talent.

"Hold it, I'm a full-figured woman and if you think one second that I'm going to becoming an anorexic sex goddess you got another thought coming."

"Rose" Alex says. "I didn't mention anything about you losing weight. I think there's nothing wrong with you being a full-figured woman. Now you're going to become a sexy full-figured woman. How will I become the sexy full-figured woman? I want you to meet Miss Sadonna Miller."

This fair-skinned long-haired beauty waltz into the office. She can give Tyra Banks and Veronica Webb a run for their money. She came to me and shook my hand while she looks at me up and down and gives me a comment "oh yes, I have a lot of work on my hands." "You see Barbrah? Sadonna is a model and a fashion consultant, she has traveled all over the world and she's been featured in the top fashion magazines. In recent years, she loaned her fashion expertise to some of the most prestigious modeling agencies in the world. You will emerge as a true rose. Time is of the essence. I'm anxious to start molding you into a diva."

I'm beginning to have some apprehensions about Miss Sadonna Miller character. She comes off real bourgeois. At the same time, I'm going to give her a chance because I'm desperate for a change. These changes are very vital to my upcoming success the same way Tina Turner had to no longer be Anna Mae Bullock. So Sadonna may be my biggest asset right now.

"You won't regret it Barbrah, Mr. Kaden shout's as I follow Sadonna out of his office."

I want to drop this girl. As we're shopping all Sadonna kept saying to me is "You must walk this way," "you say this." "you say this. Even the clothing she chose for me, aren't the clothes I would regularly wear.

"You no longer living in mediocrity but divacity." She said throughout our shopping adventure. She doesn't show mercy when it comes to my feet.

"Your feet look like a street riot occurred on them." Sadonna tells me. I'm trying on shoes now. I must prepare to catch a plane to New York to make some TV appearances. Sadonna personally hired a costume and makeup artist to help me look my best. The phone rings.

"Hello, it's your mother can you give me $1,000, I want to buy this fabulous outfit that I saw the other day.

"I don't have $1,000 to be loaning to anybody. I replied.

"You got a hit record and you're telling me that you don't have $1,000 to give me. My mom says with an attitude.

"Because I have a hit record doesn't necessarily mean I have a lot of money."

"I believe you do have the money, but you just want to give me an excuse."

"I'm not obligated to give you anything, especially someone who wasn't there for me when I was growing up. It amazes me that once I gained notoriety, you suddenly started calling. Please, I just slammed the phone. That woman only cares about herself.

New York, this city is just unbelievable. The Empire State Building, the one- or two-story Landmark is amazing. The Museum of Modern Art on West 53rd Street is the first museum I ever visit. I was blown away by the display of Martin's painting sculptures and photography. My favorite landmark so far is Greenwich Village. My goodness, I love the ambience of being around Broadway actors, artists and musicians in one area. I enjoy the interesting shops and art galleries in that area. Next is the Statue of Liberty and a Broadway play. Now I'm in Hyatt Regency Hotel eating breakfast.

"Girl, are you done eating? You better hurry up we got things to do."

That's my friend Frederique Sanchez, he's the person Sadonna hired to do my makeup and handle my apparel. He's flamboyant and gay as a goose. He wears blue contacts and wigs. He's been great company showing me around town.

When I'm with Frederique, I think of William, especially because New York is the city where he died. I miss that man so much. If he was still alive I could have helped him with his schizophrenia and we would have been married today. I'm sure that if I was on this trip with him, he would have taken me to all the fine restaurants. I thought of what a phenomenal director he would have been, his dream was to go from stageplays to tv/film, unfortunately, he chose not to live long enough to fulfill his dream. Like Brian, William died way before his time. I go to the restroom so Frederique won't see my tears. I go straight to the sink and looked in the mirror. I look like a total mess.

"Excuse me are you Barbrah Rose?' It's an overzealous heavy-set black female wearing a blue dress that is too small for her frame.

"Yes, ma'am," I answered.

"I just love your singing. It's good to see a big girl representing us for a change thank you.

I appreciate your comment."

Wow, I feel a lot better now since the lady said I represent big girls. I'm thankful that I'm still in the right mind to make an impact in somebody's life by just being me. I could have been in this same restroom vomiting my brains out trying to be super mall thing, but I choose to represent. I have a purpose, right now I'm going to go out with courage and have more fun with Frederique.

"Ok, Miss Thang let's get out of here. Where we are going next?"

"To ABC studio and I hope you didn't just call me Miss Thang."

"I sure did," Frederique says as he walks a few feet ahead of me as if he's a supermodel on a runway.

I just love the exposure that is coming my way. I have an interview with a reporter for *My World* magazine around one. Even though Soul Train was my TV debut as a performer, being on the Frank Langford show is a big deal. I'm excited. I'm performing my hit *Hypnotized by Your Love* and if there's any time left, I might perform a second song. I'm wearing this lovely short beaded red gown with a red rose in my hair. I may be invited to sit and chat with Mr. Lankford. If not, I will remain content with just being on the program doing what I love to do.

"Ladies and gentlemen singing her hit *Hypnotized by Your Love,* I present to you the sensational Barbrah Rose."

I came out in the midst of applause. I stood behind the mic and performed my hit record live before a studio audience and the entire nation. After my performance, the audience gave me a standing ovation.

Mr. Langford wearing a two-piece gray suit approached me and shook my hand. "So, Miss Rose how does it feel to have an enormous hit record? He asks.

"It's exciting." Is all I managed to say in the midst of applause from the audience.

"Well, thanks for being on my show."

"It was my pleasure," I replied Mr. Langford.

Oh my god, Mr. Langford talked to me. Later, I closed the show with a rousing rendition of *I Got Rhythm.* Next, I have a radio interview with FM 360.

"This is Tippi Hooks on FM 360 and sitting here in our studio is Barbrah Rose of smash debut single *Hypnotized by Your Love,* which has made a huge impact in the music industry. So how are you feeling?"

"I feel great. I'm falling in love with the city of New York.

"And New York is falling in love with you Miss Rose."

"I haven't had a moment of sleep since I came here."

"So why did you decide to cover "Hypnotized by Your Love"? Tippi asks.

"Well as you know, Raquel Leland did the original version and when I heard it, I just fell in love with it. I recorded my version and here we are."

"As an overweight female did you expect this kind of success?"

I was told radio disc jockey Tippy Hook was tough but I will not allow that to intimidate me.

"I don't allow my size to be a stumbling block because like Chaka Khan *I'm Every Woman.*" I replied with confidence.

"Yeah, you are every woman alright. How much you weigh? 300 lbs.?" Tippi sarcastically asks.

"Let me tell you something, I might be big but I guarantee that I can satisfy any man better than these two pics you see in these fashion magazines."

"I hope that the man you're with will still be able to breathe afterwards." Tippi had the audacity to ask such a question.

"I guess your husband is finally breathing after he walked out on you after only being married for two months."

"My marriage is none of your business," Tippi says with anger in her voice.

"But you have time to be in everybody else's business."

"This is Tippi Hooks live in the studio with Barbrah Rose, we will be taking a short break."

Tippi takes her headsets off and walks out of the studio angry. I think that was a lovely interview.

CHAPTER ELEVEN

My second single *If Looks Could Kill* just hit number two on R&B charts and number 10 on the pop charts. My album is on its way to Platinum status, I just finished performing at the Caesar Palace Hotel in Las Vegas. Now, I'm in the dressing room changing my costume.

"Hey girl I just got two tickets for the Tavis Bright concert. You want to go with me?" Frederique asks me all excited.

"No Frederique, I'm tired. This tour is wearing me out."

"Come on Barbrah, Tavis is the hottest male R&B singer right now.

"Tavis Bright cannot sing. So, I will not waste my time going to his concert."

"I won't miss Tavis Bright for the world," Frederique said to me as he does the final touches on his outfit

"Yeah, you like those pretty boys. Tall, slim, light skin, curly hair and pretty eyes."

"Whatever girl, I'll see you later then."

'Bye have fun." Frederique goes out skipping out of my dressing room.

Tavis Bright looks like Al B Sure Siamese twin. I rather see David Copperfield play butterscotch than see Mr.

Bright's act. Besides, I'm ready to get out of Vegas anyway, gambling really doesn't appeal to me and the audience are also rude. I had to chastise a man for talking in the middle of my performance. Frederique, on the other hand, thinks Las Vegas is the best town on Earth. He enjoys the drag queen stage shows. One night Frederique told me he saw a Barbrah Rose impersonator at a gay club. I got one more night in this town. The next stop is Los Angeles.

Barbara there's someone outside who wants to meet you.

"Mr. Kayden, what are you still doing here? I thought you had to catch a flight after the show."

"That can wait. This person is your biggest fan and he is determined to meet you before he leaves."

"Send him in." Walks in this tall fair-skinned dude. What in the hell does he want? He looks like Kool Moe Dee with the black shades and the rest of his black attire. Is he going to say something "why don't you watch me now"? He kisses my hand, then proceeds to take off his hat and shades revealing the most gorgeous green eyes that I have ever seen realizing its Tavis Bright himself.

"Hello Miss Barbrah Rose, I'm Tavis Bright and I just saw your act, I must say you were absolutely sensational."

"Thank you for coming to see me. I said to him.

"I would like for you to join me on my upcoming tour," Tavis says to me, it's all business-like.

"Talk it over with my manager.

"Well Barbrah, I got a performance to prepare for. I will be contacting you soon. I look forward to working with you."

"Tavis you go break a leg out there."

Wow, Tavis being in my dressing room, he's totally

different from his stage persona. He's very soft-spoken. I'm kind of flattered that he came to see me perform and then invited me to participate in his tour. Compton's Daughter, a female R&B group, and Rick Lockhart is currently signed on to the tour with Tavis being the headliner. And he wants me to be a part of that tour.

I've never tried Chicken and Waffles before but the combo is absolutely scrumptious. When I first arrived in Los Angeles, I was hungry. Frederique, who is from California, insisted that I go and eat Roscoe's Chicken and Waffles. Both of us were enjoying our lunch and having a great conversation.

"So have you heard that hit new song *Give it To Me Hot* by a new singer Melanie Hill? Tavis asks.

"Yeah that's one of the songs Tavis Bright wrote for me but I turned it down."

"Why on Earth did you turn that song down like that? "Frederique flippantly asked.

"I like songs with meaningful lyrics and Tavis songs don't come across that way at all. To me, all his songs are rather distasteful."

Well, Miss Melanie is experiencing a taste of good life with Tavis songs."

'I'm sure she is but I have no regret." I replied back to Frederique.

"What about Tavis Bright that you don't like," Frederique asks me.

"I don't have anything against Mr. Bright as a person but I don't see what the big scream about him as a performer.

He has absolutely no vocal talent. Also, I don't care for the players."

"I think Tavis likes you," Frederique says as if he struck gold.

"I'm sure he does, who wouldn't want to get with this." I confidently replied.

Well, I don't.

"Whatever Frederique, if you had one minute with me, you would be straight like a drumstick."

"Girl please, you know I don't like fish."

"This fish is one of a kind, my friend. Look at your face getting all red.

"Stop talking crap and let's get out of here."

CHAPTER TWELVE

I am wiped out. It's been a whirlwind since arriving in LA. TV, radio and nightclub appearances. I haven't had time to think. I decided to head straight to my hotel room after performing at a local Club. I was going straight to bed when the phone rang.

'Hello"

"Barbrah its Tavis Bright, how are you doing.

I'm doing well. How did you get my hotel room number?"

"Baby you know I got sources," Tavis says as if he's putting on a Mack daddy act.

"Look I'm not your baby."

'You're so touchy tonight.' Tavis says with an attitude.

"If you're calling to try to pitch me another one of your songs I'm not interested."

"I don't understand why you turned my songs down because obviously, they turned out to be smash hits for Melanie Hill," Tavis says to me.

"I'm happy for you both. I, on the other hand, must maintain standards and unfortunately, your songs don't meet my standards."

"How will someone like you have the balls to tell me

Tavis Bright, who will rock your world all night, that my songs don't meet your standards? I can guarantee that Melanie Hill will be the biggest female star in the music market because of my songs."

"Please, Melanie Hill's range is as small as my pinky finger."

"And you're as big as the new mansion I bought in Hollywood." Tavis boldly says to me. He's close to getting a beat down through this telephone.

"That's alright. I can sing your a** under that mansion." I slammed the phone hard, who does this bastard think he is. That conversation confirms how incompatible we are as musical partners. And another thing is I can't stand that fraudulent laugh of his.

It feels good to finally have a break. After touring nonstop, I have two weeks off before I travel to Amsterdam where I am booked for several performances. In the meantime, I'm going to enjoy the new mansion I bought recently in Stone Mountain. One of these days, I'm going to hire an interior decorator to help me furnish it but my focus is getting that needed rest. I haven't given my telephone number to my family. I just love the caller ID system that's out now. That's my phone ringing now. What do you want Frederique?

"I have some bad news Barbara."

"What's going on?"

"I have HIV.

Immediately I was overcome with anguish. I've lost many of my friends to the AIDS virus. Particularly my gay friends. It just breaks my heart that my best friend has to suffer this life-threatening disease. Frederique has become everything Gretchen used to be to me. I just can't bear to lose another friend.

"Wow, Frederique I really hate to hear this."

'Don't be all down Barbrah it's not a death sentence."

"Just do what is necessary to remain healthy AIDS is a terrible disease." I have to come to terms that Frederique may depart this Earth soon.

I need to get out of this house just to get my mind off of what happened. I jumped into my 98 Chevrolet and head out to the park and look down at the lake. I remember when the AIDS epidemic came out in the 1980s, people were dropping like flies, especially in the gay community.

I decided to drive to Stone Mountain Park and sit by the lake. I needed to bask in the serenity of the lake just to get my mind off Frederique contracting HIV. As I sat by the lake, two black guys approached me. They were both wearing dark color baggy pants. The dark-skinned guy smiled at me showing his gold teeth.

"How you are doing?" He asked me.

"I'm fine," I replied him.

"We want to take you somewhere." The short fair-skinned one says to me.

"I'm not going anywhere with both of you," I said with an attitude. Then the guy with the gold teeth pulls out a gun and points it at me, and hid it in his pocket so others will not recognize it.

"Look you're coming with us on a special trip. Now get up!" He yells as I abruptly stood up.

"If not, he'll have to use my little friend to take you out." The other one mentions.

Oh my God. What are they getting ready to do to me? I did what I was instructed to do and allow these criminals to lead me to a dark four-door sedan with tinted windows. They made me get into the back seat; the guy with the gun sitting beside me. The other one got behind the wheel.

"Where are you taking me to?" I asked nervously.

"Shut up!" The guy with the gun yells at me.

Then we arrived at a vacant lot. They both get out of the car. The driver of the vehicle gets on a cell phone immediately. I could not hear what they were saying. With them being out of the car, I noticed that the key was in the ignition. I jumped to the front seat and turned the car on. The abductors jumped to the front of the vehicle as I drove off. I tried to drive over them. My goal was to kill both of them but they jumped out of the way. I drove to the police station and the entire police department could not believe that I was able to escape with my life. I told them where it happened and what they look like. With me having the vehicle, they should be able to capture them in no time.

Chapter Thirteen

Since Williams's death, my dating life has been non-existent. It's not that I haven't received any offers. I receive many requests from many pursuers and admirers, but I have to reject them due to the demands of my career. Now that I have time off, I decided to allow SaDonna to set me up on a date. I'm here at CenterPoint restaurant waiting on my date.

"Hi, are you Barbrah?"

"Yes I am and who are you?" I asked the gentleman.

"I'm Herbert Tilton, nice to finally meet you. Sadonna has told me so much about you."

What is this? Who has Sadonna set me up with? So much for Prince and Shining Armor. Rather a slimy frog on a rustic cutting board. Black coke bottle glasses, with a non-descript gray two-piece suit. His pants was 3 inches above his shoes, and I know this dude isn't wearing mismatched socks. I'm going to kill Sadonna for this.

"My goodness, you're everything SaDonna said you are and much more. Herbert says to me." I wish I could say the same thing about him.

"Well, Mr. Herbert this is a nice restaurant. I've never been here before." I said.

"Sadonna told me about this place," Herbert says as he puts a napkin around his neck.

"How long have you known Sadonna?" I asked.

'I met Sadonna five years ago when she did a commercial for my company HerbTech Inc. It's a technology company I started 7 years ago while attending Georgia Tech. Herb Tech is on the cutting edge of computer technology. I and my associates are currently working on a project that will usher in a new phase in the computer industry."

That's it. Sadonna is officially on my hit list. This dude is boring. All he does throughout the evening is talking about himself and his career. If I hear anything else about computers, I might hang myself.

"What in the hell were you thinking when you set me up with that dude? I asked Sadonna as I barged into her office.

"How dare you barge into my office like this?" SaDonna says as she hangs up the phone.

"Cut the crap. How could you send me up with that man not only is he unattractive but he's boring as hell? Besides, I like men who are interesting and attractive to the eyes like I am."

"Okay Barbrah let's be realistic you are not attractive to the eyes at all. You're lucky to have a man like Herbert spend the evening with you."

"Let me tell you something sweetheart, I might be a full-figured woman, but I have all kinds of men asking me out; models, CEOs, construction workers, mechanics, etc. I bet you that if I was in the White House President Clinton would try to get with this. So, don't get it twisted."

"Look Barbara, I'm sorry if Herbert wasn't everything

Shaun Gresham

you expected but I caution you to be careful with these pretty boys that asked you out."

"Why do you want me to be cautious?" I asked with an attitude.

"Because I've seen how guy's especially "pretty boys" use women like yourself," Sadonna says to me.

"Honey, Miss Barbrah knows how to handle men who try to get over on me. I'm the last person you should worry about concerning pretty boys. Now Mr. Herbert is a definite No-No. All he did was talk about himself and his company."

"I'm sorry to hear that Barbrah and I promise I will never set you up with a man like Herbert again okay."

I've always had to deal with people's condescending attitude towards me about my figure. Despite having a mother who constantly belittles me about my body, I had to develop a thick skin. I always knew that if I can obtain a gay man. I know I can try all kinds of other men. I can keep them warm at night.

The response to performance for me on a Sunday morning church service is totally different from the response of audience at a secular venue.

"You better sing," "Praise Him", "Sing girl," these are some of the phrases from the church crowd. Now, I got Bravo and a continuous thunderous standing ovation. But the Sierra Leone incident hasn't left my memory. I still have to deal with insecure performers. When I opened for R&B singer Magic John at a concert hall in New Jersey, he had to stage curtain close on me. Now I leave the West End stage during a standing ovation. I head towards my dressing room, when I arrived, Janice McClure was standing by the

82

door. Janice McClure is a consummate soul singer who began her career in the 1980s one R&B hit after the next. I think she had two or three songs to cross over into the pop charts. In the 90s as a result of slow record sales, she moved to London where she had a strong following. Londoners have a strong affinity for black performers. I'm so glad Janice decided to come visit me. I just added her version of *Kiss Me until Dawn* to my repertoire. I hope she likes my rendition.

Hello Miss Barbara Rose. Janice says as she steps into my dressing room as if she's a royal Queen.

"Hello Miss McClure thank you so much for coming to my performance, I enjoyed your music."

"I want you to stop singing my damn song," Janice says in a curt tone.

"You're talking about *Kiss Me Until Dawn?*" I asked her as I stood up.

"Yes, that's my song sweetheart and don't you ever sing it again," Janice says as she steps closer to me

"First of all, I respect you and all, but you don't have the right to tell me what not to sing. Second *Kiss me Until Dawn* is not your song, Nat Thomas Hart did the original version so step out of my way."

"You fat cow, I wish you never came here. Your voice is too big and you're grossly overweight." Janice has the gall to say that to me.

"I may be overweight and I may have a big voice but my album is double platinum and I just received my third encore so I think I'm going to do *Kiss me Until Dawn* now.

Janice McClure abruptly walked away, I care less about her and her opinions about me

Chapter Fourteen

"Hey Sandra, how you doing?"

"I'm doing great. Preparing to perform at the Blue Strip Gardens.

"I am so proud of you girl you persevered and conquered your way to the top."

"Thanks Sandra, it seems like you and the girls are continuing to fly."

"You must not have heard the news," Sandra says to me

"What news?" I asked

"Taste' has broken up. Sierra Leone is going to pursue a solo career."

"Oh my God, I'm sorry to hear that Sandra."

"Don't be, I saw it coming. The more Paul Haynes focuses on Sierra Leone, the more disposable I and Mona became. The last three albums, I and Mona didn't sing on them. The company brought in the studio group High Imagination to record our parts. During interviews, all the questions were directed at Sierra Leone. I and Mona no longer had a voice. No opinions about our outfits and songs in that matter. Dealing with Sierra Leone was next to impossible. She became even more egotistical. Now she'll be able to bask in the glory of solo stardom."

It seems like Sierra Leone reaps the benefits of being a soloist for a while.

"It's just hard. I, Mona and Sierra Leone started as best girlfriends, now it seems like we're distant coworkers." Sandra says.

"So what's going to happen to you and Mona?" I asked Sandra.

"Mona is going for drug rehab to get over her Vicodin addiction and get the needed help. She always hated the image Paul tries to make us into. She thought of Taste' sound as being plastic and phony. On top of that, she and Sierra Leone are constantly fighting and bickering. Paul didn't like Mona having lesbian affairs. Mona has had a rough life."

"So Sandra what are your plans?"

"Either move into Hollywood and become an actress or settle down and start a family. Yeah, I can't wait to have a husband and kids.

Girl every week the media have you linked with some of the most handsome men in the industry."

I told her. "Whatever girl, I wish half of those headlines were true."

"Next week in the National Enquirer, Barbrah Rose and Tiny Tim are lovers." Sandra jokingly replied me.

"Oh, you got jokes. You're with Arsenio Hall now." I said to Sandra.

"Don't keep a secret, it will be all over the National Enquirer in no time. Sandra says to me laughingly.

Anyway if you need anything, I'm here for you. I hate that you and Mona was put into this back burner just like that.

"Don't worry about me, I'll be just fine. Sierra Leone will sure enough be your competition soon. I'm not worried about Miss Sierra Leone.

"Okay Bobbi, I'll talk to you later."

Wow, Sierra Leone going solo. I saw that coming five years ago when I was on tour with Taste'. Sierra Leone was acting like everything revolved around her even back then. Paul Haynes was pushing her further away from her singing partners. As far as her being my competition, please. Sierra Leone isn't hitting on a canned tuna. If I am to compete with anybody, it will be my contemporaries like Mary J Blige and Faith Evans. Sierra Leone vocally doesn't compare to these two ladies. Also, unlike Sierra Leone, I don't have to sleep my way to the top. I was raised to be a lady. Speaking of sleep, I could use a nap after my long flight from England, but I got some meetings to attend. I had to fire Alex Kaden because I found out that he was saying negative things about me to the media, so I got to spend a few hours speaking to some potential managers. Highlight Records sold my record contract to Surebound Records one of the biggest record labels in the world. A few years ago I approached their A&R director, he told me that my sound was outdated. The A&R director they have now can't wait to get me into the studio. As I wait at the Hartsfield Airport for my limo, a Caucasian female who looks like she stepped out of the cover of Vogue approached me.

"You will look even prettier if you lost all that extra weight." She says to me in her European accent.

"I am pretty regardless of my size." She better recognize.

When I got home, I got a call from the Stone Mountain Police Department. After the kidnapping incident the police were able to arrest my two adductors. Both were on parole. But the clincher of all this was finding out that those guys who tried to kidnap me were hired by Tavis Bright. The two kidnappers told police that Tavis hired them not to kill me but to scare me. I guess Travis had a big problem in me rejecting his songs. This is going to be in the headline news big time.

CHAPTER FIFTEEN

I decided to hire Thurgood Molineux as my new manager. Thurgood manages superstar actress Julie Mays and Haley Swanson, as well as pop star Joe Styles. He also worked with legendary entertainer Sugar Cookie and TV star Hanson Hooker. I am excited to be one of his clients. Also, I'm looking at some songs for my new album. After two years, my first album went triple-platinum and sales. I want my next album to be a stretch from the first one but my new record company wants me to keep the sound for my first album, but I don't like duplicating old sound that I had before. I'm always looking for ways to expand myself as a recording artist. I will be recording a duet with rock star Runo. I'm headed to Valley Gardens in LA to rehearse for the national AIDS charity ball that they're good booking for the last minute. People such as Elizabeth Taylor and Tom Cruise will be in attendance, then my cell phone rings.

"Hello."

"You neglected God. Now your family. It would be nice if we heard from you occasionally." Aunt Kat said to me in frustration.

"Your mother has a nervous breakdown and she's in the hospital." She continues to say.

"How did the breakdown come about?" I asked Aunt Kat.

"Your mama struggled to become a famous singer and it's hard for her to see what you are accomplishing in a short period of time in your career."

"Aunt Kat you always taught me that you reap what you sow and mama is reaping what she has sown."

"Young lady that is still your mama regardless. The Bible says honor your mother and father so your days may be long."

"And the Bible also tells us Aunt Katherine that's parents must love their children and all my life my mother never loved me like a mother should love a child."

"Your mother is in the hospital and she needs you. So, I suggest you get over the vendetta you have against her."

"What does she need from me, Aunt Kat?" All she cares about is being a part of my Success not me as a person.

"What will profit a man if he gains the whole world and loses his own soul, get that through your head young lady." Aunt Kat sternly says.

"No, you tell that to my mama the next time you talk to her bye!"

I don't have time to deal with my mother right now. She brought all the emotional baggage she's going through on to herself. It's not my fault she never had the success I'm experiencing. I'm not going to let her downfall get me down. I refuse to apologize for my success. I don't care what scripture Aunt Kat tries to quote. I'm really looking forward to the charity ball. I believe Thurgood Molineux will continue to open bigger doors for me. My limo finally arrives. Valley Gardens here I come. When I entered the building, I was immediately amazed at the Grandeur of the place, indeed this place is set up like a garden but in an elegant scale with small white tables everywhere. The small trees and plants are to die for. I love the Rose Garden almost to the point that I grabbed a few of the roses and place them in my purse. I'm sure that the paintings that hung on the wall cost more than my house. My dressing room is so in Norman's ranch-style 3-bedroom house, I heard this loud noise outside. Low and behold it was Mr. Hellmann's sitting by the street corner belting the Blues.

> *I may have silver*
> *I may have gold*
> *I turn my back on my family and that's cold*
> *The world knows my name*
> *They turn they're back on me and that's a shame.* Oh brother,

it's him again. I can't seem to get away from him it seems.

The charity ball was a great success, I performed *Over the Rainbow* and the All-Star crowd gave me a thunderous standing ovation. The celebrities were out in force tonight. I had the pleasure to chat with Will Smith, Ricky Martin and George Clooney. New singer Christina Aguilera came to me saying how big of a fan she was. Robin Williams is hilarious, and I was in total awe when I met the legendary Elizabeth Taylor. Now I'm on the airplane heading to Vegas. Before Frederique contracted HIV he moved there. He's been in love with the city since I performed there several months ago. Now I'm going to see how my friend is doing. I've been worried about him lately, so I must see him. When I get to Frederique's hospital room, I could not believe the way he was looking. The Frederique I once knew is gone. He lay in his hospital bed looking emaciated. The disease has eaten him to almost nothing. As he was resting, I diligently tried to prevent myself from breaking down. Then he finally wakes up.

"Hey Miss Rosie, how long have you been here?" He says sounding groggily.

"I've been here only a few minutes. I just had to come by and see my best friend."

"But unfortunately, it had to be in this god-awful place. Most importantly, what's been going on with you?" Frederique asks as he elevates himself from the bed and sits in a chair but barely managing to move.

"Well, I hired a new manager and I came straight here after performing at a charity ball last night in LA. I tell you, I met all kinds of celebrities. I dedicated and performed Over the Rainbow to you".

"Thank you Barbrah, I wish I was there to see it". Frederique says in tears.

"Now, don't you go crying on me," I said to him as I went closer and held him in my arms.

"I just wish my life turned out differently, what would have happened if I had not been molested when I was 7 years old he says in anguish."

"You never told me you were molested, Frederique.

"My uncle molested me from the age of seven to the age of 12 when my family moved us from Puerto Rico to LA. I thought it was a normal part of life until the age of 16 when Oprah Winfrey started talking about her molestation. By that time, I was living a life of promiscuity sleeping with other guys. I was even selling my body for money."

"What did your parents say about this?" I asked my friend.

"I came out to my mother when I was 18 and my father left the family when I was five."

"Have your mother come to see you since you've been in the hospital?"

"Unfortunately, since I came out my entire family abandoned me. I tried calling them, but they won't return any of my calls."

Frederique, I'm so sorry to hear that."

"This gay lifestyle is painful. The gay friends I used to party with stop having anything to do with me because of my ill health. There were with me during the partying days but nowhere around me in time of sickness."

"Well, I apologize for not being here sooner.' I said to Frederique holding him tightly.

"I know you love me, Miss Rosie," Frederique says like a child.

"Yes I do and I'm going to make sure you get better."

"Well, I know one person who's not doing better. Mr. Tavis Bright." Frederique says.

"Oh yes, how could that fool do that to me just because I rejected his songs," I reply to him.

"I'm going to start calling you Pam Grier with your bad self." Frederique laughingly says before he starts to cough very hard. I approached him and started patting his back.

"You better watch it, don't laugh too hard," I say to him

"I don't know anybody who would've escaped a situation like that alive, except you," added Frederique.

"Look sweetie, I got to get out of here," I say as I kiss Frederique on his forehead.

"Okay, I'll see you later." Frederique sadly reply as I leave.

CHAPTER SIXTEEN

It's October and my new album entitled, *Living the Life,* was released to the public. I'm very excited about it. It has more of an urban hip hop Edge to it than my first album. I worked with Kissy "felony" Atman's and Rocaword the most innovative songwriting team in the music business today. Henry Donaldson the CEO of my record label is very excited about my album. But when he suggested that I record a song called *I'll Be Your Only Other Woman* written by songwriter Marilyn Jones, due to the content of the lyrics. I was shocked when I realized that the song is about a woman who is very committed to being a married man's mistress. One of the lyrics in the song says, you aren't going to get it for free and you aren't going to buy for cheap. The song is the first single released from the album. Even though the song has climbed to the top of the R&B charts, I only performed the song live a few times. I'm preparing to headline my first tour which will last two months.

I keep in contact with Frederique whose back home now after refusing to live in the hospice and refusing to move to Atlanta to live with me. I did hire a nurse to take care of my friend. I'm basically the only family he has left even though he's gotten back in contact with his sister and brother.

I just finished a promotional concert at Tower Records when people came out in droves. I was famished and I decide to go incognito and grab a good meal at Helen Soul Food and Grill. 1949, Helen Wilson a recently divorced mother of three children converted a burnt down nightclub into a restaurant. Establishment has become a staple point in the entertainment community. People like Oscar Peterson, Liza Minnelli, N'Sync and Nancy Reagan have eaten here. The moment I stepped foot into the restaurant, the aroma of the food captured me. It's almost intoxicating, especially because I'm a lover of food. As I looked around, I saw that the restaurant has no frills look to it. I asked the waitress to give me a glass of warm water as I continue to peruse the menu. Suddenly, an elderly female with salt and pepper hair wig wearing a white apron over a blue dress approached my table. I'm trying hard not to laugh at her coke bottle glasses.

"Hey baby, I'm Lena Wilson. I'm so glad you finally came by. I still maintain contact with your mother. She's one of the greats. I remember having to babysit you when your mother performed at the Apollo Theater. You were a little bitty ole thang."

"Wow, that's quite interesting to hear". I said to Miss Wilson.

"Your mother regret some of the choices she's made especially concerning you." Miss Wilson says to me.

"What do you mean Miss Wilson?

"All I'm saying baby is for you to please forgive her." Miss Wilson pleadingly stated.

"Look Ms. Wilson no disrespect but I don't want to talk about my mother," I flippantly said to Miss Wilson.

"Remember sweetie, your parents love you so much and so do I." Miss Wilson says to me in a motherly tone.

"You know what, make my order to go. I got to get out of here." I said as I collected my purse. I went from famished to being irritated. I might treat myself to a shopping spree. The waitress brings my food and I left a $10 tip.

"You come back to see me." Miss Wilson yells out as I left the restaurant.

When I arrived at my hotel room, there's a message on my voicemail and it's from Frederique and nurse. Miss Rosie, I have some bad news. Frederique passed away an hour ago. Please call me as soon as possible. My day couldn't get any worse, but I knew the time was coming. Frederique, 29 years old of age is gone. A man so full of life dead of AIDS. I bawl over in tears for two hours before I called Cynthia.

I'm at Rob Taylor's funeral home in Las Vegas where I just finished burying Frederique. It was a happy home going service. Nurse Cynthia told me that Frederique simply took a nap and never woke up and with her help, I contact all his friends and loved ones. I performed *Over the Rainbow* and *Precious Lord* which was two of Frederique's favorite songs for me to sing and he said that if I don't perform the song he was going to come and hunt me down. He wanted to be cremated. I stood in the parlor as people got in their vehicles to leave. A Hispanic man and woman approached me.

"Hi, are you Barbrah Rose," the lady asked me.

"Yes, I am," I replied.

"I'm Frederique's sister Maria and this is our brother Patrick."

"Thank you so much for taking care of my brother, you were such a great friend to him," Patrick says as he shakes my hand.

"Yes, we got back in contact with each other two months ago. We came and visit him, and we talked every day until his death" Maria says.

"Yes, we have so many regrets on how we treated him," Patrick says sadly.

"But I'm so glad that Frederique gave his life to the Lord. Patrick happily states.

"Hallelujah," Maria exclaims. "That's one of the best things that happened since we reconnected with Frederique. He asked us how he could be saved, and we were able to lead him to the Lord. I give God all the glory for that."

"Amen," I said. Before they get on this Hallelujah trip, I dismissed myself.

"It was so nice finally meeting the both of you. Frederique was elated that he was back in communication with the both of you. He will remain in our hearts forever. I got a flight to catch."

As I was about to leave, Marie taps me on my shoulder. And God has plans for you too Barbrah Rose."

Chapter Seventeen

"Hello Bobbi, it's your Aunt Kat. The doctor diagnosed your mother with breast cancer. Please call me, we all miss you. Wow, my mother has breast cancer. I will call them later. It's three months into the new millennium and I'm still touring to support my second album. The record company released a club remix of the single *I Will Be Your Only Other Woman* which has climbed the top of the dance charts. My following with the gays is stronger since the single release. And I also attribute that to my relationship with Frederique. He's probably up there looking down on me. In recent weeks, I performed in a gay club and they know how to cater to a diva. Most of my gay friends were friends with Frederique. At the same time, I'm still judgmental towards them because of their lifestyle. They always tell me that they were born that way. I don't know because I'm not in their shoes. But I know they love themselves some Barbrah Rose.

"Hey, babe are you coming to bed."

"Yeah, I'll be right up," I answered back.

That's my new boyfriend Damian Hendrix. I met him at a nightclub in Atlanta where I was performing. He came and asked me for my number, and we've been dating ever since. He has an exotic-look, especially because he is from an African American father and an Asian mother. He got good looks and he's not so bad in the bed department. He's very tall and muscular with a megawatt smile. He's an entree that I constantly enjoy. If only Sadonna could see me now. I really haven't seen her since I fired Mr. Kaden.

"Hey baby, I was wondering how long you were going to keep me waiting," Damien says to me looking like he just stepped off the cover of a romance novel.

"There's no way I'm going to keep you hanging," I say to him as he wraps his arms around me.

"Now give me those lips," I say as we both kiss passionately.

"Hey girl what's popping?" Penny asks me as I step into the dressing room studio.

"Lack of rest is what's popping my friend. The record executives at my record company is pressuring me to record a hit selling album after sales lagged on my last album." I said to her as I sat down on the chair to get my makeup done.

"Don't worry about that. You still working. The company can't do anything to you." Penny tries to admonish me. "They can drop me from their roster, and I don't want to go through that ever again," I said to her.

That's Penelope "Penny" Bolden I'm conversing with. She's a white girl I hired to take Frederique place after he became ill. She stands 4 foot 9 and loves black men. She's always telling me once you go black, you never go back. She's very comedic, constantly making me laugh in stitches.

"What record company was crazy enough to drop you?" she asks me.

"Climax Records."

Shaun Gresham

"You're talking about that label located in Atlanta. They had a full-figured singer named Bobbi Minor several years ago. You kind of remind me of her." Penny says that she put the last few touches on my face.

"It's smart to save and invest your money. I'm learning that it is not about how much money you make, It's about how much you save.

"Oh, you trying to be Oprah Winfrey," Penny says to me.

"No, it's about growing and learning. I'm trying hard to educate myself on finances. I even subscribed to Forbes Magazine. I don't want to be touring at the age of 50." Then the phone rings.

"Is Damien girl," Penny says as if she Shaniqua at a Burger King Drive-Thru.

"Hey baby."

"Hey honey, what are you doing?" Damien asks.

"Getting ready to perform on Hit Town video show. What are you doing?" I asked.

"Laying here waiting on you to get back." He replied in a sexy tone.

"You know I'll be back in 2 days. So, you better have that house cleaned before I get back. All right?"

'You know I'll Be Missing You." Damien says to me as if he's an infant.

"I miss you too. I got to go. I'll call you later okay?"

"Girl, you got a man on locked?"

"Oh, shut up. He's a good man but the only problem I have with him is that he doesn't have a job." I said to Penny.

"What kind of work has he done before?" Penny asks.

"Modeling."

"Oh Lord. Models are the laziest people I have ever met in my life. Believe me, I'm dated one. They rely on their looks, eschewing jobs that require hard labor so be careful Miss Barbrah," Penny says.

My house is totally messed up. Crap all over the floor. I'm going to let Damien have it. It's ridiculous how my house is looking.

"Damien?! Where are you!?"

"Hey babe." Damien answered as I barged into the bedroom. His butt was still in bed.

"Don't hey baby me! What in the world happened to my house! It's a mess!" I yelled as I kicked an empty beer can.

"I'm sorry sweetie. I had a couple of friends over to watch the game and we got carried away. I'll clean the house later."

"No, you're going to get your lazy a** up and clean my house right now! It doesn't make any sense for my house to look like this. Another thing, when are you going to find a job?!"

"Look, you should stop yelling and let me get a little more rest?" Damien says as he tries to conjure up a puppy face.

"No, clean up my house damn it!" I screamed in fury.

"Baby please I'm sorry. I promise I will clean everything up."

This man sounds so sexy when he apologizes. He walked towards me to nibble my ear.

"It's been two days since I saw you. We got some catching up to do." He continues.

"Hey don't go there." I firmly said to Damien.

Come on sweet Rosie. All right. I'm going to allow Mr.

Damien to sweet talk me into love land. But don't think for one minute he's going to get away with not cleaning my house. The doorbell rings.

Don't answer the door baby. Damien says as he continues to nibble my ear. I will be right back.

"Who is it?" I shouted.

"It's Gwendolyn Hendrix, I'm looking for Damien." I immediately opened the door.

"Who are you?" Gwendolyn asked me in a sassy tone.

"I'm Barbrah, Damien's girlfriend."

"What, I can't believe this; I've been his wife for the last nine months," Gwendolyn says confusingly.

"Oh, hell no! Damien get out here now! I yelled in anger.

"Gwendolyn, what are you doing here?" Damien says sounding all casual.

"You no-good for nothing bastard, I had to find out from your friends that you're living here now. But I didn't know you were living with another woman." Gwendolyn shouts as she begins hitting Damien with her purse.

While Damien and Gwendolyn were in the living room arguing, I immediately went and packed Damien's belongings. I should have known something like this would occur. I can't believe I wasted my time on a married man.

"Alright Mr. Hendrix, get your crap and get the hell out of my house. You can go back to your wife Miss Gwendolyn." I said to Damien as I threw his belongings at him.

"Oh no girlfriend, he's not coming back with me. I've had enough of this lousy man." Gwendolyn says to me with her hands on her hips.

"Barbara please don't do me like that, I love you." Damien conjures up saying to me.

"Save the drama for your mama dude, you're just low down. Get out of my house." I said to him.

"The thing we do as women to get a man. Gwendolyn explains as she leaves. Damien walked behind her begging her to take him back.

I sit on the sofa thinking of what just happened. The only thing Damien had going on is dashing pretty boy looks. He never took me out. He never bought me gifts. All he did was mooch off me. I can't believe I settled for a guy like that. Like Gwendolyn said, things we women have to do to get a man.

CHAPTER EIGHTEEN

"Come on Barbrah, I need you to focus. Tonight is a big night. So, come and get the program!"

I am three seconds close to slapping the piss out of Mr. Molineux. All he does lately is yell at me. I've been dealing with the pressures of giving a great performance for Mr. Molineux, and producing a platinum selling album for Elliot Goodman, the multimillionaire CEO of Surebound Records. He's taken a big interest in my career since the low sales of my last album. My next album will be released close to my birthday. After that, I'm going to take a much-needed break. In the meantime, I'm at Yellowstone Park rehearsing for their upcoming Spring Festival. My heart isn't in it at all. I still can't get Damien out of my mind.

"Mr. Molineux, my heart isn't in it today. Can we cancel the rest of the rehearsal and go home?" I ask with melancholy and exhaustion.

"Tell me what's going on Bobbi?" Mr. Molineux asks me in a fatherly tone.

"I'm tired of giving my heart, only to be stump upon by these no-good men," I answered before I broke down in tears. Mr. Molineux came and wrapped his arm around me.

"Don't let that guy get you down. The right one will

come along and sweep you away. There's plenty of carpets to choose from" he says.

"Mr. Molineux," I laughingly said, "there's not enough carpet in the world that would sway me off the sausage."

"I can easily set you up with Rosie O'Donnell," Mr. Molineux says.

"That's okay, Mr. Molineux, I'm nowhere near that desperate for love."

We went to the Stones Bar and Grill, a little drive fifteen minutes away from the park. I only saw one black face amongst the Caucasian crowd.

"I'm looking for a new love baby"

"A New love.......... yeah…. yeah…. yeah"

That voice sounds familiar to me. I turned around and it's Robert "Bluesman" Hellman singing a blues version of Jody Whatley's *I'm Looking of a New Love.* That man is still wailing into the new millennium.

"Do you know him?" I asked Mr. Molineux.

"Who doesn't know Mr. Hellman? That man is a legend. He always performs at the least likely places when you least expect him." Mr. Molineux says as he sips his beer. What I love about Hellman is his ability to draw people whether he's singing on a street corner or a huge stadium."

"What stadiums have that man performed at?" I ask as I chump down on my hot wings.

"Years ago, the Rolling Stones invited him to be an opening on one of their world tours. I was one of the promoters on the tour. I tell you, that man was fantastic."

"The Rolling Stones are old fossils still touring all year round," I tell Mr. Molineux.

"I need to book you on one of their tours." Mr. Molineux says to me.

"Oh no, Mick Jagger would be trying to get up on all of this. Did he do a song called *Brown Sugar* which is about his fascination with black females?"

My cell phone rings.

"That's Aunt Kat calling me again. She wants me to come home and visit my parents."

"You need to go visit them. You only get one mother and father." Mr. Molineux tells me.

"My mother has breast cancer and I haven't seen her yet."

"What are you waiting on Barbrah? You can't be so caught up in these men and your career that you neglect the important things in life." Mr. Molineux preached to me.

"But they neglected me all my life. Now my mother has cancer and suddenly I'm supposed to inconvenience myself for people who never inconvenienced themselves for me." I said to Mr. Molineux as I get frustrated.

"They are your parents regardless of how they treated you in the past. Take it from Mr. Molineux, we as parents are not perfect."

CHAPTER NINETEEN

This house hasn't changed too much after almost 10 years. I'm back in Raycliffe, Georgia to see my family. Really, I'm here because of Aunt Kat's prodding and begging me to come back. Since getting the breast cancer diagnosis, my parents moved back to Raycliffe to be close to family. I being a dutiful daughter will visit them even though they were not dutiful parents. Also, this visit is a fulfillment of the promise I made to myself. When I left Raycliff as a teenager, I told myself that I won't return until I became a superstar. Now I'm at Platinum selling recording artist, no longer the gospel chirp of yesteryear. There might be a parade in my honor in a few days.

"Look what the cat drug in," a voice behind me to says.

"Look what the cat left behind", I say back to my sister Benita.

"Miss Big Time Star in our midst," Benita says to me in a sarcastic tone.

"So how are you Benita?" I asked trying my best to be civil because I really don't want to deal with her.

"Busy tending to our mother." Benita frustratingly says putting her hands on her hips.

The relationship between Benita and I has not been

great. She is two years younger and was raised by her parents. Named after our dad's brother Benjamin, she had the benefit of growing up in the glitz and glamour of show business. I, on the other hand, was stuck in small-town Raycliff under the religious fervor of Aunt Kat. Benita has always been considered the pretty one and I the chubby cute one. My mother treats her like she's God's gift to the Earth, but always telling me I need to go on a diet. When they visit Aunt Kat and me when I was growing up, they would both look at me with so much disdain. And don't get me started on Benita singing ability. She sounds like a brillo pad scrubbing on a frying pan but my parents have spent thousands on her fledgling singing career.

"Benita?" I asked her how it feels to live in the sweet countryside of Raycliff. I bet its hard-getting caviar on these side of the Hills."

"Bobbi," Benita says, it will be nice of you to pitch in to take care of my mother. I and Dad have been doing all the work while you travel the world basking in superstardom."

"There's my baby," Aunt Kat says as she walks into the house defusing the tension for a moment. We immediately walked towards each other and embraced. Aunt Kat has gotten a little gray in her hair. Also, she's a little slimmer than she was when I left Raycliff. she was wearing her dirty work uniform, she continued to work there for the past fifteen years.

"Thank you Jesus my baby girl has made it home," Aunt Kat says as she holds me beaming.

You need to tell your baby that she needs to release some of that celebrity star money towards the care of her mother. Benita has the nerve to say as Aunt Kat restrained me from clocking her.

"Aunt Kat"? I asked, can you pray for me. Pray that I don't cuss anybody out and act all out during my visit here."

"Bobbi Tots," Aunt Kat says, we are not going to have that at all in this house. Now I'm going to cook you up a feast that will put Piccadilly to shame.

"How come you didn't cook us a feast when we came here?" Benita asks Aunt Kat.

Aunt Kat ignores her and goes upstairs to her room. Benita is really getting on my nerves and apparently Aunt Kat's.

"Mother is upstairs in her room waiting anxiously to see you," she says to me. "I have to go get her medicine" she continues as she walks out the door.

Thank you, Jesus she's gone. Now I got to go see Deborah. She and Howard decide to temporarily move into Aunt Kat's house, so they will be closer to family while Deborah gets cancer treatment. I made the dreaded walk upstairs which I haven't walked in several years. I got to Deborah's and Howard's room which is a room Aunt Kat uses for guests. I'm hesitant to open the door. When I opened the door, the room was completely dark.

"Deborah," "it's me Bobbi."

"Bobbi I'm so glad you came. Your father is visiting some friends right now." Deborah says as she turns the light on. Deborah has a scarf wrapped around her head. I'm sure she has lost a lot of her hair due to the cancer treatment that she's getting.

"How was your flight," she asked.

"It was pretty nice, especially flying first class. Oh yes,

flying first class is awesome, Deborah says. Have you seen your sister, she continues.

"I saw her," I said dismissively.

"Bobbi!" Deborah yells. "That is your sister, you can't treat her like that."

"No, she needs to stop thinking that she's better than folks looks like the chairs has turned." I confidently States.

"Bobbi I don't want us to be arguing. I'm sorry I haven't been a good mother to you. I'm sorry for all the times I wasn't there for you when you were growing up. I'm sorry I prioritize myself over everything including you and your sister."

As my mother was saying all these things, I was in a flood of tears. I went and sat on the left seat next to the bed and Deborah came over and held me in her arms.

"I and your father have given our hearts to Jesus. Please forgive us Bobbi." Deborah continues to say while holding me.

"Bobbi?" Aunt Kat asked as she walks into the room, are you okay?

"She's doing just fine. God is answering our prayers, Katherine." Deborah assuredly says as she wiped the tears from my eyes.

"Well dinner is ready," Aunt Kat says, and she wipes her hands on her apron

"Rub-a-Dub-Dub I'm ready for the grub," I said as the three of us laughingly head to the kitchen.

Aunt Kat went all out with the fried chicken, macaroni and cheese, spaghetti and meatballs, green beans, mashed potatoes, cube steak, and all kinds of food that is good for the soul. I haven't eaten this good in almost a decade.

The awesome part of all this is that I, Aunt Kat, Deborah, Howard, and even Benita sat down at the same table and had dinner together. Seems like better things are to come for my family.

CHAPTER TWENTY

I'm at Aunt Kat's house amongst family and friends after a busy day. She threw down with the food of course. This day has been mind-blowing, the day began with the parade in my honor downtown Raycliffe high school cheerleader and drill team as well as several local dance teams. Seeing all the welcome home Barbara status hanging around was awesome. In the afternoon, I had lunch with the mayor and his family in the mayor's Mansion. The dates included at the Tilton Auditorium we have soundstage with my parents and believe that along with some City officials looking out into the audience. It is full. The RayCliffe High School band treated the audience to Renditions of some of my hit songs. I even perform for them. Then I was presented with a handmade key to the city.

"Bobbi, you are a blessed person." Aunt Iola says to me as she fixes her a plate of food. She is now as thin as a whistle after having gastric bypass surgery. She even tried to encourage me to go through the procedure but I'm kind of apprehensive about it.

"Thank you, Aunt Iola, for being here," I said to her.

"You need to know that your mom never had a parade in this town in her honor." Uncle Hester says. He and my

Aunt Iola have been married for almost 20 years. They live in Augusta Georgia, where they run an insurance company

"I'm just grateful that this occasion brought so many family and friends together," I mentioned back to him. Things are turning around for me and my mother since we had our talk. Even Howard is interacting with me more than he has in the past years.

"Yes, it's been 10 years since we all been in one place at one time," Aunt Josephine says. She lives in Nashville Tennessee where she's a featured vocalist on BET's *Tommy Johnson Gospel Hour.* Tommy Johnson's a staple in the black gospel world period. In fact, Josephine has been trying to get me to appear on the program for years.

"Yes, child it's been a long time since we performed together," Aunt Lucinda says joining in the conversation. "I feel a reunion coming on. The last time we were together was at one of Deborah's concerts when we did a gospel medley."

Lucinda is single living life as a hair salon owner in Savannah.

"I think somebody needs to help the Sisters get a record deal," Lucinda says staring at me.

"I'm sure Deborah can work that out for you all," I deflect. One of the downfalls of being a celebrity is that people especially family constantly approached you, wanting you to give them a handout.

"Hello ladies," Bishop Collins says as he suddenly appears putting his arm around me. The climate of the room shifts. My aunts were giving each other funny looking stairs.

"Bishop Collins?" Deborah asks. "What on Earth are

you doing here?" He and Deborah's relationship has been contentious for years for some reason.

"I'm here to celebrate our daughter's success." Bishop Collins tells Deborah.

"Daughter's success what the hell are you talking about Bishop?" I ask in fury as I removed his arm from my neck.

"This is not the time or the place Bishop," Deborah yells.

"It's time for her to know Deborah," Bishop tells her.

"Know what?" I asked in frustration and confusion.

"Bobbi sweetheart." Bishop Collins says. "I'm your real father."

"Deborah is this true," I asked in tears. "Is this lying, lowdown worm of a Preacher Man my father?" The house became so quiet that you could hear a rat pee on cotton. Deborah is in tears now and all eyes on the three of us. I'm waiting for Deborah to answer me.

"Answer me Deborah is Bishop Collins my father?!" I yelled angrily.

"Yes Bobbi, Bishop Collins is your father. I dated him briefly before I met Howard. When I met Howard, I was already pregnant with you. I am so sorry."

"Really! So, my whole damn life has been a lie. To find this out on this day of all days, I said in front of everybody.

"Baby girl," Bishop Collins says.

"Don't baby girl me!" I yelled as I ran upstairs to my room. I started to pack my things. My life is shattered. Now I'm beginning to see the light. Howard Minor is not my father that's why he didn't stay around to raise me. That's why he has always been distant towards me, but lavish so much love on Benita who is my half-sister. Bishop Collins a married man hooked up with my mother. Which resulted in me being born in shame. Which caused my mother to leave me in the care of Aunt Kat. While she went into the world of entertainment. Bishop Collins the Man of God continued to teach chastity and purity to his congregation, I must depart from this town of lies. I'm recalling all those times Aunt Kat called me yelling at me concerning how I treated Bishop Collins because she knew he's my father. I might as well put a BC sign on myself. Bastard Child. I will never return to this town again. I feel like I'm a joke.

It's September a few months after my homecoming parade fiasco. Bishop Collins with his megawatts smile and fake preaching vernacular has gone to the media and told the entire world that I am his daughter. While all this was going on, my latest album was released. I had the toughest time recording and Mr. Goodman couldn't agree with what songs would be good for the album. There were times when I thought the album was finished but Mr. Goodman would make me go back into the studio and record a dozen more songs. It almost came to a point where I wanted to give up. But I'm relieved it's finally done. *A Rose in a Hard Place* is the title of my new album. That title couldn't be any truer in my life right now. I haven't had any contact with any of my family members despite them trying to contact me via letters through my fan club. I changed my telephone number. Deborah and Benita even had the nerve to show up at one of my concerts, but I did not allow them into my dressing room. I just can't be bothered with them right now. I thought things were turning around for good in my family. I just can't deal with the drama right now.

I'm at the grocery store Incognito in the produce section. Suddenly, I saw a white female walking towards the meat section. I looked a little closer and realized that it's my old friend Gretchen Fanning. I immediately approached her.

"Hi Gretchen," I said to her.

"Bobbi oh my God!" Gretchen says almost yelling as we hugged each other.

It's been five years since we saw each other. We stopped talking to each other after the Antonio Wilson incident. I hope to God that she's not with that loser anymore.

"So how have you been girl?" I asked Gretchen.

"I'm doing pretty well. I'm a recent divorcee and a mother to two kids." Gretchen answers.

"You got two kids and still got a body like that," I say to her as I walk around her staring her up and down. "You have always been the type that doesn't gain any weight but eat everything you want. But If I look at a piece of Pound Cake, I'll gain five pounds." I continued to tell her as we both began to holler in laughter.

"Yes, I got a 4-year-old son Joseph and a two-year-old daughter named Samantha."

"I'm so glad things turned out well for you. Do you still dance?"

"No, I sure don't. My ex-husband didn't allow me to dance. Once we got married, he demanded that I give up everything I love doing and be a housewife. So, are you still performing?" Gretchen asks me.

"Yes, I do but do you know what I call myself these days? I asked Gretchen. I'm sure she knows who I am despite me wearing this get up.

"I'm Barbara Rose nationally-known platinum-selling

recording artists," I whispered to Gretchen because I did not want to draw attention to myself from the shoppers.

"Wow, congrats I really don't listen to music that much especially with me being a mother now. But I'll go to the record store and get some of your music. You are such a talented performer."

Gretchen's life has changed in the last few years. She married an African American man named James McCalep, a doctor who owns a family practice in Alpharetta, Georgia. They divorced because of James' involvement in Scientology. Gretchen didn't give me much details, but she told me that they were employing too much control over how they should live their lives. Gretchen has never been the type to get involved in cult religions. She must now raise her kids as a single mother. She has some rough days ahead of her, but she will persevere.

I feel so good to have some time off. *A Rose and a Hard Place* album has gone Platinum and I will be touring at the beginning of the new year to promote it. I am in my pajamas no makeup with my hair in a simple ponytail. I'm in a total relaxation mode. I looked at my bookshelf to find something to read. Then the King James Bible suddenly fell from the Shelf. I haven't touched a Bible in years.

"Bobbi give your life to me." I hear this voice say to me suddenly, I wondered where it was coming from.

"I am the Lord, and I'm requesting your life, your talents, your mind, and your soul." I was nervous to death as I heard this voice again. I didn't know whether I'm supposed to run out of there or not.

"Okay Lord show me if this is truly you.

A fresh wind suddenly blew. Okay, it's really the Lord.

What must I do? I need to go to church. Tomorrow will be Wednesday, and I'm sure there will be a church service going on somewhere. I turned on the television to get my mind off from what just happened. Renown preacher S.C Gaines appeared on the screen and made a heartfelt speech.

"At the sound of my voice, there is someone out there who is required right now to surrender. You have no choice in the matter. You tried doing it your way, but you're not happy. You got the fame and fortune, but you are not happy. Jesus wants to give your life and life more abundantly." This man is talking to me.

"If that's you, I want you to repeat this prayer after me." SC Gaines continues.

Jesus come into my heart. Forgive me for my sins. I believe that you died on the cross for my sins. Cleanse me Jesus. Make me into a new creature. Thank You Jesus for coming into my life and making me whole.

With tears in my eyes, I repeated everything that Pastor Gaines said. I felt an immediate change occurring. My life will never be the same. All I can do is praise Him.

Chapter Twenty One

"You're not the same person Bobbi," Penny says to me as she places makeup on my face.

"You went on hiatus one way and came back a child of God." Alfred, one of my security guard, says making quotation marks with his fingers.

I am at the Apollo Theater in preparation to perform in the first concert of my 3-month tour. God is awesome. I gave my life to Jesus Christ of Nazareth. I didn't do anything for months but study the Bible. When I gave my heart to Christ, I felt a weight lifted off from me. The Bible does say old things have passed away; all things are new. Christ is no longer the person my Aunt Kat knows but a risen Savior I'm experiencing myself day by day.

"Bobbi, you look so different," Penny says to me. "Did you apply some moisturizer or something on your skin?"

"That's all God," I replied. "It's the Lord's doing and it's marvelous in my eyes." I continued to state.

"It's the Lord's doing, Penny," Alfred says with his hands clasped together as if he's praying the mother Mary of the Catholic service.

"And it's marvelous in my eyes," Penny adds her two cents as she does a phony ballet dance.

"Look, joke all you want," I said to both of them. "I'm in shock at the way you guys are behaving. I didn't plan this; it's God's doing."

Both Penny and Alfred began to roll their eyes. They are not the first people to experience my rebirth. Mr. Molineux is a total skeptic concerning Christ. He became concerned when I told him that I might not renew my recording contract with Surebound Records when it expires in a few months. My life is no longer my own.

"You're up at five minutes Miss Rose." The stage manager announced. I began to feel nervous. I'm no longer the person who wants to please my audience but please God.

So far, my set has been fantastic. The audience responded with thunderous Applause. As I prepared to go into my next song, I heard a commotion going on at the back of the theater. Lo and behold, I saw Sierra Leone walking towards the stage. Sierra Leone is the reigning Queen of Pop. Most music publications have declared me the reigning Queen of R&B. My main competitor in the music business as far as record sales is Sierra Leone. Kind of like Aretha Franklin and Dionne Warwick back in their heyday. Her extracurricular activities with drugs have been in the headlines in recent months.

"Give it up for the Queen of Pop Sierra Leone," I announced to the crowd as they continue to go wild.

When Sierra Leon stepped in front of me, she began to speak in a raspy scratchy voice. "Isn't she the best? She asks the crowd.

"Yes." They exclaimed.

She began to sing Precious Lord, and I sang harmony as we shared one mic. The audience went crazy, but Sierra

Leone's voice is totally ravaged by constant drug usage. When we finished, Sierra Leone hugged me and departed the stage like the diva that she is. "Give it up for Sierra Leone," I said to the crowd.

My show was complete. I went to my dressing room, and standing there was Bishop Collins with his arms out wide grinning.

"What do you want?" I asked him frustratingly as I wipe the makeup off my face.

"Is that how you greet your father?" He has the nerve to ask with an attitude.

"Father? You don't care about me as a child; what you did to me at the homecoming is self-serving. It wasn't about you cultivating a relationship with me. It's all about celebrity and prestige for you."

"I've known you all your life. I'm not a stranger to you. My blood runs through your veins!" Bishop Collins yells

This man is pissing me off. What does he want? He's all about himself.

"I want a blood test," I said to him.

"Fine, you will get one." He says as he leaves my presence.

My old carnal man would've cursed Bishop Collins out. But I'm no longer that person anymore. I'm a sinner saved by the Blood of the Lamb.

CHAPTER TWENTY-TWO

It's 2:15 p.m. in Boston, Massachusetts, at the Royal Marriott Hotel. I'm here for the third performance of my tour. I just finished watching Remember the Titans while eating a scrumptious lunch. I turned the TV to the news, and I got shocking information.

Pop music Superstar Sierra Leone is dead at the age of 29.

"What!?" I screamed as I jumped out of bed and began pacing around my hotel room. I can't believe that Sierra Leone is no longer here. Her body was found on the floor of the Trump Towers Hotel in her room. I started to think about the history we had years ago at climax records. Her kicking me off the Taste' tour as their opening act. Despite her limited vocal ability, she was a diva and a superstar.

"Bobbi, have you heard about Sierra Leone? Mr. Molineux asks me with his cell phone to his ear.

"Yeah, I just heard it on the news," I responded.

"I'm getting calls from the media requesting an interview with you." Mr. Molineux tells me.

"Why do they want to talk to me."

"They're saying that Sierra Leone's last public performance was at the Apollo Theater three days ago."

I thought about her coming on stage as I performed

that night her way of apologizing to me for getting kicked off the Taste' tour. I need to contact Paul Haynes as well as her former group members Sandra Duncan and Mona Latimore. My cell phone is ringing off the hook.

"Here, the contract to model for Jane Holland clothing store." Mr. Molineux says as he hands me what looked like a book to sign. Jane Holland is a clothing store for plus size women. I couldn't pay them to come my way years ago when I was Bobbi Minor. Ever since I became Barbrah Rose, I've had many opportunities. From hair products to electronic gadgets, I can't tell you how many production companies that approached me to do a reality TV show. Then Mr. Molineux hands me a large certified letter. I believe its Bishop Collins DNA results. I opened it and Hallelujah; thank You Jesus, Bishop Collins is 99.99 percent not my father. I picked up the phone and call Deborah.

It's been months since I spoke with her.

"Deborah, the DNA says Bishop Collins is not my father. Who is?"

"What, I can't believe it. Deborah says in shock."

"Who is my father, Deborah?" All I heard was silence from Deborah. "Look," I said. "I don't have time for this mess. You have done a lot of damage in life, so it is best you tell me who my father is."

"His name is Caleb Higgins," Deborah says almost in a whisper.

"Are you talking about the soul singer Caleb Higgins?" I asked Deborah. She became reminiscent. I met him in 1972 when I and your aunts performed at a revival meeting, Caleb's father was preaching. The Revival was in a small backwoods town in Mississippi; we did a couple of songs with Caleb. I tell you, he knocked the crowd off their feet. While his father was preaching, we went out to eat at IHOP, eventually ending the night at the Holiday Inn. That was the only time we had intercourse.

Wow, all this is mind-blowing—I kind of looked forward to meeting him.

"Are you still in contact with him?" I asked.

"The last time I saw him was back in the early 80s. He was appearing at a rundown juke joint in Chicago not too far from where I was appearing. Like many singers who starred in church, he tried to cross over into secular music, but Caleb could not get his career off the ground." Deborah recalls.

'Vocally, Caleb reminds me of Donny Hathaway." I told Deborah. I bought a reissue compilation CD of all his recordings a few years ago.

"The last news I heard about him is that he returned to the church," Deborah mentions.

"Deborah, I need to find Caleb. Thank you."

There is a possibility that Caleb Higgins could be my father. He was born in Memphis, Tennessee, where he started singing in the church. His father was a traveling evangelist for a lot of years. He was discovered at a talent contest in Nashville, Tennessee. He was signed to Epic Records and recorded three albums for them. Deborah even sang backup in one of them. He also had the opportunity to record in Muscle Shoals, Alabama. But his whereabouts today is unknown. I will have to hire a private investigator to find him.

CHAPTER TWENTY-THREE

I'm at New Life Missionary Baptist Church, which is a mega church in Atlanta for Sierra Leone's funeral. Paul Haynes personally contacted and asked me to sing Precious Lord. The church was crowded to capacity. I discovered that Sandra Duncan has made it, but no one has heard from Mona Lattimore. I'm still sad about Sierra Leone's death. She passed away from a drug overdose. It is rumored that she and Paul Haynes were separated. I was seated near the pulpit area with other celebrities. The funeral began.

The choir ushers in the presence of God with *Lord I Lift Your Name on High*. As they were singing, Mona Lattimore finally appears and gave me a big hug. She looked very ladylike in her black dress. I thought Mona would have passed away from a drug overdose, not Sierra Leone. By her appearance, Mona looks like she has conquered that demon.

Next on the funeral program were some words from the funeral organizers as well as the pastor of the church. Now it's my turn. Lord anoint my vocals. Draw all men as I lift you up. As I walked to the pulpit, Frederique came to mind because I did Precious Lord at his funeral. I told the pianist to play as I started singing.

Precious Lord take my hand

Lead me on, let me stand
I am tired I am weak, I'm lone
Through the storm, through the night
Lead me on to the light.
Take my hand precious Lord, lead me home

I sang to the glory of God, which caused a praise break to occur. One of the touching moments of the funeral was when Sandra and Mona said a few words together regarding their relationship with Sierra Leone. There was a lot of tension among those girls when they broke up, it was good and that they all reconcile before Sierra Leone's death. There were a lot of other celebrities who spoke and celebrated Sierra Leone's life.

The private investigators I hired located Caleb Higgins. Who lives in Nashville, Tennessee, where he does studio session work. He is also the minister of Music at a local COGIC Church. I'm standing here at his house in a neighborhood that is not different from the neighborhood I grew up in. I am so nervous now. I stood at Caleb's house, wearing a grey mink coat in the freezing cold. One person that's crestfallen about all of this is Bishop Collins. He didn't want to know me for who I am but for what I got. He thought he could get close to me and live off my fortune. I'm sure his church attendance will reduce once they find out that I'm not his daughter. I on the other hand, could care less. It will not bother me if I never heard from him again. I knocked on the door. A gentleman with salt and pepper hair opens the door.

"Hello, can I help you?" The man asks.

"I'm here to see Mr. Caleb Higgins?"

"This is him."

"My name is Barbara Minor. I'm here to tell you that I may be your daughter." Caleb stood there staring at me as if I have lost my mind. Did I do the right thing by coming here?

"Is this a joke? First thing I'm going to tell you young lady is that I cannot have children."

"I am absolutely sorry Mr. Caleb. I don't want anything from you but to find out if you're my father. This is not a joke. If you can do me a favor by taking a DNA test."

"Who's your mother?" Caleb asks me.

"Deborah Toombs"

"Oh yes, I remember Debbie," Caleb says as he invites me in his home. You could tell that the house belongs to a singer. What stood out to me about the house was the grand piano in the living room with sheet music scattered all over it. "She and her sisters used to blow folks out with their singing. In fact, I used to sing with your Aunt Josephine on the *Tommy Johnson Gospel Hour*. How old are you Barbrah?" He asks.

"I'm 28."

"Yep, you could probably be my child because Debbie and I had one encounter about 28 years ago. Let's do a DNA test. It will be a miracle from God if I have a child."

"Mr. Caleb," I said. "I know this is not easy for you, but I have been going through a journey for several months concerning this issue. I just found out about you two weeks ago. The man I thought was my father was always distant towards me. I just want to know where I come from."

"I'm so sorry Barbrah that you had to go through all of that. If I had known that you were my child, I would've been a part of raising you. So, what kind of work do you do Barbara?"

"I'm a singer."

"I guess the apple doesn't fall far from the tree on that one." Caleb laughingly states. It may have fallen from two trees because Caleb is a formidable vocalist himself besides possibly being my father.

"Are you a gospel singer?" Caleb seriously asks me.

"No, I'm the R&B singer going by the name of Barbrah Rose." I felt comfortable enough to tell this man who I was.

"The world famous Barbrah Rose. Wow, I love the early blues and jazz recordings that you did with Climax records."

This man knows my previous recording history. We ended up talking for two hours. We will do the DNA test, and we promised to meet each other in person very soon. Father in Jesus name, let this man be my dad.

CHAPTER TWENTY-FOUR

It feels weird to be back in Raycliffe, Georgia. After that fiasco that occurred at my homecoming, I promised myself I would not return here ever again. But Christ has gotten a hold of me, so therefore, I must make things right with my family. I'm at Aunt Kat's house to see her and Deborah. It's been months since I saw Aunt Kat.

"There's my baby girl." Aunt Kat says to me as she comes down the stairs.

"You look like you lost a few pounds," I mentioned to her. I recall back in the late 1980s, she got the Dick Gregory diet powder shake for herself and me. We lost a tremendous amount of weight. I think that was the only time I can recall Deborah ever being proud of me.

"I've been doing portion control and not eating past 7 p.m. The doctors even decreased the amount of medication I take. Thank God for Jesus." Aunt Kat exclaims.

I sat down looking around the living room, the plastic cover brown sofa set, the antique coffee table that was bequeathed from a grand-aunt, the family Holy Bible located at the center of it and a green telephone that is older than me. I'm trying to get Aunt Kat to buy a cell phone, but she refused to get one. Pictures of me, my aunt, and my grandparents' covers the entire wall. Then there's the grand Brown piano. Aunt kat can play it like nobody's business. I remember spending many afternoons with her on that practice in numerous songs. Deborah came down the steps and hugged me; she looks quite different.

"You're looking quite refreshed," I commented.

"Yes, I do because I no longer have cancer!" She says as if she's going to Disneyland. That's great; I said as I hugged her.

"God is good," Aunt Kat testifies as she sits on the sofa. "So, what brings you here?" She asks.

"Well, first, I must tell you that Caleb Higgins is my father." We are both ecstatic about the news.

The day I got the DNA results will remain one of the best days of my life. Caleb called me in tears after he read the results. He thought he would never have kids. He started calling me his miracle baby.

"Caleb Higgins? That name rings a bell. Did we sing at some revivals for him and his dad years ago?" Aunt Kat asked Deborah.

"Yes, we sure did," Deborah says pensively.

"I'm so happy for you baby," Aunt Kat says that she pats my hand. "It would have been better if he was around when you were growing up."

Aunt Kat is starting to get all riled up. She's always preaching on the importance of a man being there for his child. She used to give Howard hell about how he was treating me when I was growing up.

"Aunt Kat," I said. "He didn't know I existed until a few weeks ago." Aunt Kat looked at Deborah shaking her head while Deborah looked down in shame. Aunt Kat used to be hard on Deborah due to her promiscuous ways back in the day.

"The second reason I'm here is because I want to work on my relationship with Deborah," I said to her as I held her hand. "Because I'm in Christ now and I want things to be right between us."

"Am I'm hearing you right?" Aunt Kat asks. "You're telling us that you gave your life to Jesus Christ."

"Yes ma'am." I'm grateful to God for this woman. She's been crying travailing and interceding for me all my life. As I look back on my childhood, Aunt Kat would go on a fast. No television, phone, magazines, friends or food. Just water and constant prayers, and the results speak for itself today.

"Hallelujah! Thank you, Jesus!" Aunt Kat begins to testify. "Thank you, Jesus, for answered prayers." Deborah remained seated, showing no emotion concerning my rebirth. Aunt Kat, on the other hand, went to the piano and started playing it.

"We had some times at this piano." She mentions to me.

"Oh yes, *I Surrender All* was the first song you taught me on this piano when I was five years old. I told her. Aunt Kat then starts to sing it.

All to Jesus I surrender
All to Him I freely give
I will ever love and trust Him
In His presence daily live
All to Jesus I surrender
Humbly at His feet I bow
Worldly pleasures all forsaken
Take me, Jesus, take me now,

Her strong raspy contralto resonates as Deborah and I join her. I think this is the first time Deborah and I will be singing together. All three of us rejoiced together in the Lord, singing wonderful songs to His name.

CHAPTER TWENTY-FIVE

"I Should Be Your Only Other woman!"
   "Give it to You Straight!
   "I'm Looking for a New Love!"

The crowd is going wild here tonight. I'm doing a one-night-only performance here at the Ribs & Bones Café to complete my obligations with Mr. Molineux. He's pissed off with me. I really don't have the heart to do a whole concert. For several months, I've been looking at the lyrics of the songs that I've been singing. They're contradicting with my newfound beliefs.

My record contract with Surebound Records has expired and I didn't choose to renew my contract. Now I'm sort of a free agent. Mr. Molineux wants me to continue singing secular songs. He thinks of me being a follower of Christ Jesus a joke. My heart desires is to know my Lord and Savior. I'm no longer bound to man's opinions. I continued to search for a church home, and I continued to be an avid reader of the Word of God. I went into a state of melancholy when I was booked to perform at a nightclub. I looked at the faces of the patrons; I saw the emptiness and the lost that they possess. I was also empty and lost but now I have peace, the peace that no night club can give me.

I heard the Spirit of God saying sing *Great is Thy Faithfulness*. At first, I was afraid but then that scripture where it says the Lord hasn't given you a spirit of fear but of love, power and a sound mind comes to my mind. As a Christian, it's my obligation to bring the love of Christ to a place of Darkness. After all, Jesus commanded his disciples to go out into the world with the gospel.

Great is Thy faithfulness
O God my Father
There is no shadow of turning with Thee
Thou changest not
Thy compassions they fail not
As Thou hast been
Thou forever will be

I'm sure that the crowd desires to drink, dance and hear me sing my secular hits songs, but I saw their hands lifted towards heaven with tears coming down their face. My band, which some of its members was raised in the church, was shocked when I began singing the hymn. But they begin to accompany me. A worship experience occurred right there. I led many of those club-goers to the Lord. To God be the glory for He does excellent things.

The concert went well with the audience. When I arrived in my dressing room, I released a huge sigh of relief. Thank you, Jesus. Not by power nor by might but by your spirit. I thank you for the hearts that were changed. Yokes were destroyed and burdens lifted, I give you all the honor and glory on tonight.

As I praised God, Mr. Hellmann approaches me in tears. He looked like an angel. His cloths are not ruddy looking. He no longer has several teeth missing. He no longer looks like the dude I always see singing on the street corner.

"Baby girl, I enjoyed your singing tonight too. I felt the anointing of God. I used to be a gospel singer. And Great is Thy Faithfulness is my favorite gospel song. Girl, God put you in my heart and I have been praying for you for years. Now, I got to go. Okay?"

"Yes sir."

As he walked out, I wondered how he went from being a gospel singer to singing the blues. The business can be that way sometimes. On top of the world one minute and out the next minute. It also happened to me. A rising singing star on the jazz circuit, a year later no record label but by the grace of God. I believed that what I do for Him will last.

Chapter Twenty-Six

"Good morning, High Praise Church of God in Christ, how can I help you?"

My life continues to go in full circle. I'm back in the church in more ways than one. I returned to the church that I attended while growing up, which is COGIC. But this time in Nashville, Tennessee. Because I wanted to be closer to Caleb. We saw each other almost every day. I even met his three sisters, my aunts Betty Jean, Joan, Claudette and his brother, my uncle Jacob.

Things between me and Deborah are still shaky. She's jealous that Caleb and I have grown close. But she's the one who withheld the info from me. So, I put her in God's hands.

After that night at the Ribs & Bones 5 years ago, I left my career behind. I moved to Nashville, and with Caleb's help, I got a job as a receptionist at High Praise and on Sundays, I'm their praise and worship leader. I also supplement my income by giving voice lessons and studio work. I'm no longer bound to gain the things of this world. When I meet Jesus on Judgment Day I want him to tell me well-done you good and faithful servant. I lost 50 pounds and continuing the journey with obesity. But according to the word of God, I'm fearfully and wonderfully made.

"Hey Bobbi."

"Benita! What are you doing here?!"

I came to surprise you. I'm here for a Mary Kay convention.

What a surprise indeed this is. Benita and I have come a long way in our relationship leaps and bounds. There is no longer any contention between us. After my rebirth, Benita gave her life to Christ, which has brought us closer. Now she's having issues with Deborah as well as her father Howard because she's no longer at their beck and call. She's become her own person.

"Oh my God, I can't believe you are here. I said as I hug my sister. "Tell me how's married life treating you." I continued.

Benita Minor is now Benita Barker. Her husband Tyus is a project manager at LAX. They met in LA when Benita came there for a Mary Kay Convention. She's been one of their biggest distributors for years. She loves life in LA, which the cost of living is high for me.

"I want to take my big sister out to lunch," Benita says.

"And you know I don't say no to free food," I comment as I went to get my purse.

Benita took me to eat at Chuck's Steakhouse for lunch to catch up. The restaurant is located near the Grand Ole Opry, which is a legendary country music venue. All the great country music stars have appeared there.

"So, how're things going with your love life? Benita asks as she chows down on her steak."

"It's totally non-existent," I answered. "But it will all

happen in God's timing. One thing I won't do is chase after a dude. A man that findeth a wife has found a good thing."

"Amen to that," Benita agrees. "I can sure say that about Tyus. When he saw me for the first time, he pursued me relentlessly.'

I've been celibate for five years since my rebirth. It's not easy when it comes to dating, especially when you have a relationship with God. Being a Christian is sometimes a turnoff to most men. One thing I won't do is relinquish my God for romance.

I see a man contacting you to work on a gospel project. Benita prophesies.

Benita has acquired a gift of Prophecy, a gift that is massively strong in our family. Benita has spoken a lot of stuff into my life that has come to pass. So, I'm not a stranger to the spirit of Prophecy. In fact, that goes on a lot at St Paul. Suddenly my cell phone rings, and an unknown number shows up. Benita went to the restroom, so I answered the call.

"Hello, is this Bobbi?"

"Yes, it is."

"This is Tim Gray."

"Tim Gray from Climax Records?"

"Yes ma'am."

This is crazy. I haven't had any contact with Tim for probably a decade or more.

"I'm calling you Bobbi because Paul Hayes and I wants to do a gospel project with you. We're both followers of Christ now, and we want to use our gifts to advance His kingdom."

After Sierra Leone's death, Paul Haynes went through

a downward spiral. He numbs his pain with alcohol; then someone invited him to a church service. The minister at the service preached a life-changing message on salvation, causing Paul to give his life to the Lord. This in turn, led Tim to salvation a few weeks later.

"Girl, another one of your prophecies has come to pass." I'll tell Benita when she returns from the restroom. As that old gospel song says, I wouldn't trade anything for my journey now.

Printed in the United States
By Bookmasters